The Funhouse

Fernando Alegría

Translated by Stephen Kessler

Arte Público Press
Houston

This volume is made possible through a grant from the National Endowment for the Arts, a federal agency.

Arte Público Press
University of Houston
University Park
Houston, Texas 77004

All rights reserved.
Copyright © 1986, by Fernando Alegría
ISBN 934770-52-2
LC 85-073355

Printed in the United States of America

The Hunt

One day, or rather an afternoon, when everything's done and no more footsteps are heard in the halls and instead that stale smell of foul air, clothes and cigarettes which is the breath of offices and elevators hangs there, and the yellow lights go slowly white and the campanile lets loose a few clangs into the still cold fall and, in short, something is happening which is time passing—a blue time that lasts just a moment, turning to a pink glow—the professor is talking with a student.

The professor is a tall, slow-moving man with a large head of long dark-blond hair and big sleepy blue eyes, and he's leaning a little over the young man as if throwing a wing around his shoulders, not touching but covering him, because the young man seems to be made of something insubstantial, and there's a purely virgin pleasure, a quiet enthusiasm moving inside everything awakening in the world at that hour, and this tanned youth, in shirtsleeves, with a wide-open face and thick eyebrows and a smiling mouth, his hands folded under his chin, is looking into that other ruddy face, the hairy forearm and fingers gesturing and settling down around a pipe; both drawing rhythmic truths from common things (outside, a bench; inside, books, the ashtray, the clock, a portrait; outside, a yellow truck passing, two old people holding hands at the edge of darkness, a shadowy gardener sinking his arms into the earth), not out loud but in soft harmonies, waves which embrace both teacher and student like beautiful swimmers in the golden sun, and life suddenly takes on a deep sweetness and an unknown feeling, clear and pure, passes through the two faces into their throats and expands and illumines them, and nothing is happening—the clock has stopped—and through the windows, open two by two, a gust of wind blows in from the eucalyptus: a revelation is about to occur.

Then silently the door opens. Someone dressed like a hunter appears. His glasses gleam. He's holding a rifle. He takes aim hastily and fires. The blast opens a hole in the young man's back and through this hole a violent spurt of thick dark blood comes gushing. The hunter fires again and this time the shot tears off the professor's face. In the office there's a single eye left open, lonely, observing.

The hunter goes out, shuts the door and runs to the nearest newsstand. He buys a paper, scans the headlines, gets impatient, reads the classifieds, the personals. Desperate, he throws down the paper, goes in person to take out an ad. He writes:

"This afternoon's act of war was performed for free. I'll return the bodies with medals."

He tears up this ad and places another:

"God is out to lunch. He'll be back to count the dead."

The House

When I first got here I felt uneasy. I don't know these people's language, they smell funny, their pushiness and prejudices make me sick. It feels like I'm coming into a huge cage hanging from a cherry tree in bloom; it's spring and a cool wind is moving the clouds over the fields and fountains, and the sky with its blue eye follows me through the crowd, all the way down the platform, and watches me get into a yellow cab.

Men and women are jostling in the darkness, trampling each other, attacking each other on the buses and trains. An ambulance pulls up in front of a movie theater and collects the wounded. But there are wounded in the restaurants too. I know which streets to avoid: heavily armed muggers are on the loose.

Still, it's spring and the city lights up its monuments at dusk, and in the bell towers, in the bronze gates, in the white cement archways, in the parks' iron railings, an air of madness and the murmur of a thaw are building.

What's going on? It's a city at war: the papers speak of hunger, of treason and rape and of old people doing maneuvers in the snow, the women wear brass knuckles and pedestrians lie bleeding under the bushes.

The driver barks, takes my money and tosses it on the floor, then he takes out a chain and ties up his car.

But now I'm in a nice street with brick houses, moss-green,

damp with some kind of rain or inner sweat. I don't see a soul. The street-lamps are covered with paper bags. The windows painted black. I direct my steps toward a big iron door where I see the number I'm looking for. I rap with the old lion's paw knocker and wait.

A long time passes. Night has fallen. All this green thickness of creepers, rhododendrons and lilacs covers me with its coat of musty leaves. I feel the water dripping off my hat and sliding down my back. Suddenly I notice a hand signaling from a distant balcony, just a very white hand, and perhaps a black shawl, in the darkness. I push open the door and step inside with my suitcase splashing in the puddles and bumping along the loose stones.

Now I'm facing a steel door spotted with dried blood. I wait a few minutes. It opens and I enter a dark vestibule. A lively and cheerful very old woman's voice invites me in. It's my boss. She says a few clipped words. She laughs. I can't see her but I feel her presence and breathe her vinegar smell. I take a few steps and she takes my hand, leading me. We walk like that a long while in the dark along what must be a bridge or corridor. I smell some sort of dust of carpets or plush furniture, an air of flowerpots and plastic flowers. I'm having a hard time breathing. I want to let go of that hand and go back to the street and soak with the plants and trees and cuddle up to the covered streetlamps. But the old woman keeps up the pace, and then we're at another door. It's an elevator, also dark. The woman opens it, makes me go in.

"Get off where the elevator stops," she tells me, "and look for your room. Take this," (she hands me a box of matches), "there's no light in this house, the war, you know."

"But aren't you going up with me?"

"What for? There are plenty of people upstairs, you won't be short of company. Besides, the doors here don't have keys."

The elevator grill shuts and I go up slowly, I don't know how many floors, I can't tell how big this elevator is, I don't know if there's anyone else in here with me. It could be that this is a little iron cage and I'm stuck here for good. A long time goes by but the sound of the gears keeps on and the darkness blackens. I don't know if I'm going past floors or just moving up a shaft. Finally the cage stops and the door opens. I step out with my suitcase and look around. I find myself in a wide, brightly lit corridor. I feel ridiculous with a burning match in my hand and I blow it out. The corridor stretches for blocks in both directions. I see endless doors, all alike. Iron numbers. I move unsurely, trying to identify voices, sounds, but I don't hear a thing. There's nobody here. Just space, lights, doors. I go on walking, I think I see the end of the corridor but it's a corner and the new corridor loses itself in lights and reflections. I get the feeling I'm in a vast maze of linoleum hallways, I know there aren't any windows, I sense there must be another floor, esplanades, squares, markets, parking lots, restaurants, theaters, barracks, and pretty soon I'm going to meet the others like me.

Even so, I'm in no hurry. I go on walking, searching, sniffing. Until I get there.

There's an open door. Slightly ajar. I go in, set down my suitcase and look around.

My family's in there: my white-haired wife, smiling sadly, and the kids in bed looking at me too. I cross the room, approaching the window. It's not really a window. It's a mirror and there we are again, a little more apprehensive, quieter, sadder. Then it hits me that I've arrived and softly I start to cry.

Rosamel and the Clockman

Now I'll tell the secrets—most of them anyway—about Veronica.

I'm talking about Rosamel, whom I've cleverly placed on the opposite side of the room. Maybe he knows he's been set up, his squinty eyes are constantly shifting, looking around but not really seeing.

What interests me now is why he took such a humiliating job (there may be differences of opinion) and why he quit and spends all his time laying around the house biting his fingernails and never leaving Veronica or me in peace. He's always bothering us, hiding behind doors, eavesdropping, spying and generally acting like a victim.

He lisps a little, not much, but he sprays spit when he speaks, his lips are thin, his whole face fine as if drawn with Chinese ink on parchment, or like a figure in a wax museum, his forehead furrowed and his scalp bald, because he's bald in spite of his youth, smoothly tanned like the handles of certain canes.

"In the first place," he says, "there was nothing else available and I really needed a job. This guy paid me fifty bucks a week. I went to work at eight at night and finished at six in the morning. During the day a nurse took care of him. He lived in an oxygen tent that had to be working constantly to keep his heart going. He was a clockman, with a pendulum, minute-hands and everything. They took him out of his metal case to oil him, clean him, wind him up, but only briefly. Under the tent he read, ate, slept, peed, shat, thought, kept quiet, made plans.

"He didn't sleep well. He had nightmares. He was especially scared, as you can imagine, that while he was sleeping the pendulum might stop and his heart too. A normal concern for a clock, you'll say. He woke up yelling so I could convince him he was still alive. And yet he was a very cultured individual. Which was strange because he'd been paralyzed since the age of five and still went through grade school and high school, earned a college degree, took a doctorate and became a professor, all from inside his clock case. He was always reading. His library consisted exclusively of erotic literature. A complete collection, the great and the worthless—the wild French, the oral English, the violent Italian, the pale Nordic, the holy and obscene of India, the palpably African—in beautiful costly editions which, though kept in glass cases, displayed the traces of time, I mean the fingerprints and stains of its spillage. He read, like I said, constantly examining the photos and illustrations, at all hours of the day and night. All of a sudden he'd call me over and bark sharp orders: Rosamel, he'd say, come scratch my crotch, son, it itches something awful, lower, harder, there, right there, like that, harder, press a little, rub, man, that's it. His day nurse did the same thing. Fifty bucks more a month for blowjobs. But not me. It's not that it was against my morals, but it struck me as an abuse of power, a way of getting revenge against vertical humanity, bending it over on all fours and giving it what it deserved. Maybe the fact that I was an exile and an outcast interested him. Because sometimes, actually quite often, I stood there looking out the window into the garden, over those smooth dark lawns and those thick hydrangeas and those white iron chairs with their colorful waterproof cushions, and seeing superimposed the image of my mother bleeding in the snow and the dogs coming up to lick her. And this guy watched me and figured fifty bucks was plenty.

"Our enemies hadn't treated me or my sister too badly, but before—what we saw before! My God! My father was fairly rich because the family owned some large vineyards and we produced as much as a third of the country's wine. But he was a Jew and during the war the Nazis killed him. My mother almost went crazy. She wouldn't talk. A few months later she remarried. At an official reception a chandelier came loose and fell on her head. My stepfather hated me from the start and once, when I was fourteen, attacked me with a knife and nearly killed me. Our enemies, like I said, respected us. They raped other people elsewhere. Us, they fed. And our relatives remembered us and, fearing we might be brainwashed, brought us here. How could I pass up my first job? I lived with the clockman a month, winding him up by hand, and I'd have stayed longer if my finger could have held out."

Rosamel shows me his thumb and forefinger, joins them together, kisses them, makes the sign of the cross and swears.

The House Again, Now Full of Hippies

All this happened in a curious world which could have been a city but in fact was a house. We lived in this house for many years. Here we came together, we separated, we hated and loved each other; here we opened up to each other like ripe fruits in beds that weren't ours; we spied on each other through skylights and keyholes; we went after each other with knives, bottles, chairs and hot irons; here Rosamel hanged himself; beautiful children were born; we held literary discussions; we conspired together on the white nights when shining Guatemala fell like a little tower; here we cried for a Jewish couple electrocuted in New York; here Cuzco was taken prisoner; here we drank hot chocolate in honor of first communions; here we were that summer night, staying up till dawn, singing, the air heavy with jasmine, and all of us dancing hand in hand, so young, not even knowing Rosamel would hang himself, that Cuzco would wind up in jail, that the Monk would go crazy and be sacrificed by the Pueblo Indians of New Mexico, that other beautiful children would come to be baptized and confirmed and some would marry in their turn and others give up religion and others go off to war, and later I'd struggle desperately, kicking and screaming, so they wouldn't lock up my wife and take my children away to be slaughtered, and that night, all of us sweetly stoned, hanging from the fences and the tree branches, the lilacs and orange blossoms and honeysuckle breathing along with us, still knowing nothing and incredibly happy, grinning, we thought we'd be here forever, unforgettable, indestructible.

 The house is the size of two city blocks and loaded with abused children, cocaine dealers, first communions at sunrise. They spread their legs in the baroque peyote arcade; they hold still, hypnotized by the soap bubble growing around the world and lighting it up with rainbow colors and draping God's belly like a belt of jewels, or like a pocket watch from whose stem a black preacher preaches while batmen hold him up sucking on his body from head to toe, and there are youngsters in the laundromats, delicate vampires trading little bells and forget-me-nots and sharpening their teeth on the sidewalk, and the Mexican dishes fly through the air like UFO's maneuvering over the Greek Theater shrouded in fog at that hour, and a few child prodigies run around the terraces offering themselves to the Chamber of Commerce, and others play chess or read the funnies or eat lumps of sugar soaked in LSD in the pee-stained loft of the old Harvard psychologist whose eyes well up with white water trying to twinkle, and everyone is calm and innocent with the fervor of the new religion born in the dawn of the hamburger stands and in the one-way flights of pizzas from Giovanni's, setting out on the trip without a worry about possible collisions with astronauts who've blasted off too just a few hours before, and the motorcycles roar under their deranged angels, Marlon Brando types with long curls and braids cruise the Mediterranean Cafe showing off the swastikas sewn to the seats of their pants and sneering at the pacifists who watch them and go on playing their flutes and their finger cymbals Ginsberg brought back from India, and a few minutes later all the police in the world will swoop down and there'll be a scuffle, chains and pool cues flying, all in a tiny space barely half a block long, a violent dance floor for a stately waltz of blue-clad, club-wielding giants and leatherey black-booted ladies and pacifist page boys with beards and big mustaches, all taking one step forward and one step back, a wild little dance on a field of false teeth, sweaters, books and shoes, all lost forever, never found.

The house I'm talking about, I'll level with you, is like a wide well-lit avenue planted with very green leafy trees in the summer, with a lovely set of tracks for streetcars that come by clattering, loud and slow, and the passengers make the trip every Sunday just for the smell of the Italian delicatessens, the five-and-tens, cafes and hardware stores, and they get off in front of the El Rey theater with its big marquee and wind up eating gigantic sandwiches smothered in mustard, standing on the corner where the Salvation Armies beat on each other to the tune of the ambulance sirens.

Agent O

I've got to find a job.

I have several offers. Since most men have gone off to the war, the Employment Office informs me I can operate elevators or ventilators or oxygen tanks; I can also be a jailer or an embalmer or an executioner, but by the same token I could be a forest ranger, I could print money, tear down houses, milk goats, pick locks, tend the headlights of subway trains, I can be a spy or lead condemned men to death through downtown streets, or stamp prostitutes' cards and give them their shots. I could preach, but I don't know the language.

First I'll be a spy. That is, I'll try to be one. I won't even have to leave this great house where I'm already starting to put down roots.

These folks who'll be my colleagues, mornings, behind their desks, under the pink neon, don't scare me. On the contrary, I sort of like them. My Bosswoman gives me thousands of blank sheets of paper and tells me to draw. She also gives me stamps and photographs and fingerprints. I'll do posters for the post office offering rewards for the heads of eminent individuals. The price for each head will be up to me. But they'll be expensive. I'd like permission to have lunch, I tell my Bosswoman. She looks me over through thick glasses. She has a little round white head and a little round body. She wears a silk blouse, red tights and black boots up to her knees. The Bosswoman detects something in my attitude.

"How many heads so far?" she asks.

"None as yet, but I have lots of ideas."

"I know what's missing and we're going to fix it right away," she says. "You need a bigger room where you and your family will feel more comfortable."

"A window," I say, "a window. That's all. I'll find room for our furniture, my books and records."

"The city's at war, don't forget. Don't ask for too much."

"I'm asking for very little."

"Where is your furniture?"

"In the street."

"Wait a minute."

She picks up the telephone and dials. She asks questions in a sharp tone, impatient. She strikes the desk with her whip. "It's in the basement now," she says. "We'll have to have a look."

But it's still in the street, in front of the iron gate, we can see it from the roof. And we can also see an old woman standing by the railing with her arms folded, blocking the way of the moving men.

It's a rainy but sunny afternoon. We wander through the gardens of the house moving with a certain slowness in a mist which rises from the asphalt and wraps around our legs. Everything seems to be breathing: the pines, the acacias, the magnolias, the dense red-leaved eugenia, the crooked old lilacs, the thick soft moss. The fountains are filling with dead birds. A bugler follows us at a distance sounding like a car horn in the woods. There are people shopping in brightly lit drugstores, getting ready for the bloody battles to come. Booksellers are dusting their shelves with white feathers.

I tell this woman that a city like this, dripping with springtime green, makes me anxious to work and that she can count on me despite the fact that I'm so lonely.

"We'll have your flat," she says, "your family will be happy."

"When? When? My wife is very upset, she writes me that she wants to come as soon as possible."

"She has to be patient. First we'll make sure they let your furniture in, then I'll help you get settled, we'll put up curtains, rugs; we'll drill a well."

"A window."

"We'll put in a window."

"And perhaps a park for the kids to play in?"

"We'll put in a park."

"Ah, if only they were here!"

"Don't get sentimental. Get tough."

"When can I tell them to come?"

"Be patient."

"I've been here for years now and they're still waiting to be sent for."

"The country's at war, everything's hard, you're not the only one who's lonely. Quit whimpering."

I found myself alone for various reasons and it was imperative that my family come, even to the darkness of this huge cage, even if we had to look at our furniture from the window, even if we didn't have a window and had to live wandering through the halls and elevators.

"A lovely city in wartime," I say to her, trying to get on her good side.

Bringing my family became an obsession. I was often surprised to find them beside me. I saw them at night, with our furniture, in the street. Unable to sleep, I got out of bed trembling, feverish, I stuck my head out through the cracks and tossed burning matches down. Little by little, like on a smokescreen, areas of the garden lit up, the railing appeared and I could see a bronze cot set up on the footpath and sitting there in her nightgown, her hair down, her eyes intense, looking at me reproachfully with a strangeness I didn't understand, was my wife, and next to her our little boy and girl, sucking their thumbs and smiling. I was tormented by the idea that it would start raining and that they'd get wet and catch cold, so I threw down some newspapers. Once I threw down bedsheets but they got caught on the powerlines.

I requested a job as a school teacher and they gave it to me.

A sense of solidarity developed in this house, but not without fears and suspicions: as teachers we had to expose ourselves to the cannibalism of the students.

I had to get up early, before seven, dragging my feet, holding up my pants, barefoot and unshaven, shuffling down the freezing hall with its lights ablaze, and shut myself up in the bathroom, sitting there thinking about my life, about the Bosswoman, massaging my stomach and planning a master class which would lead to a raise and shorter hours. Naked, with a towel around my neck, I shaved and then went out, flushing the toilet.

Still half-asleep, my little wife was making coffee and the kids in bed watched me, the girl sucking her thumb and the boy chewing on a piece of blanket. My stomach hurt.

"Woman," I said, "I must have cancer."

"How come?" she asked, making an effort to open her eyes and push the hair out of her face.

"I feel something like a golf ball in my throat."

"It's your Adam's apple."

"I also have shooting pains in my legs. Look," I said, showing her my calves, "on both legs, in exactly the same place, I have these rashes. And on my arms, too." Forearms, to be exact, in the same place, two big spots testified to what I was saying.

"It could be mange. It doesn't have to be cancer."

"It's just that this thing in my throat won't go up or down. I feel like I'm filling up with air," I added, groping my way into a chair.

My wife helped me on with my overcoat, scarf, gloves, hat; she kissed me and I went out in search of my classroom through the misty hallways. The students had tons of clothes on too. All the doors were shut and the cracks sealed. A fried smell stuck to their clothes and another smell, of leather jackets and damp wool, a smell of faces, of noses and mouths, like the smell of a stable, filled the room and made everyone nauseous. But we were asleep so we could stand it. I called the roll in a rage. Not looking at them. I recognized some of the voices: they were voices that made me furious with their impudence or their motherly tone or their smugness or their goddamned tendency to prejudge everything, including me. In other voices I sensed the possibility of doing business. In others, the certainty of it. Pia, for example.

Pia lived alone, but she hadn't always lived alone. When she was very young she'd married a veterinary student and they'd had a few months of peace and happiness.

Pia sang to herself in her Italian accent, ironing, washing, waxing, frying, boiling, cooking, cutting her husband's hair. "It didn't matter to me," she said, "if my husband did his anatomical studies on the kitchen table. That could be cleaned up, a matter of wiping it off with a wet sponge. The organs weren't clearly identified and I could make them out only when my husband explained them to me. One day there were little mole lungs or sheep kidneys, or a coyote brain or a deer stomach, or monkey breasts or a kangaroo pouch. A little blood didn't bother me. Besides, a lot of this stuff wound up in the skillet. We were fairly happy, in spite of you know what." (I knew that Pia was frigid back then.) "He understood me, and when things warmed up we ate and took a bath or resorted to our little chamber ensemble, he with his viola, I with my cello. And this calmed us down and sent us to bed exhausted. It went well. It was all going fine. But he got his degree, took out a license, became ambitious, wanted to make a lot of money, move to a bigger apartment, set up a clinic. And that's when the problems started."

Pia took a deep breath and coughed, her eyes got red and focused on my fingers, with which I was making little ducks out of breadcrumbs. "Frigidity . . .," she continued.

"Yes," I said, "tell me about frigidity."

"Frigidity isn't an individual condition." Ah. I kept my eyes on her, skeptical but not sarcastic. "It's a relation, a tension, it's a bridge. A bridge between two people. No one can ever be sure who's to blame. We both feel desire down to our fingertips, the tension is there, everything's working, the touch, the kiss, the push of legs and feet, the smell. The one who's the boldest and most understanding and who helps the most and gives the most and advises and consoles and figures everything out in order to set things straight and seems capable of doing it for both people—that's the frigid one. The other one, hot as a flame but stiff, suffering, helpless, terrified, and also full of a tremendous wave that builds but never breaks, isn't to blame for anything but being there, at that particular time and place, waiting for the lightning that's striking someplace else."

After her separation, Pia organized a rather turbulent Maoist cell in her flat. It was infiltrated by all kinds of secret government agents. This made it more popular.

"It wasn't frigidity that caused the divorce, as you might think," she said. She sat on the floor of that dark apartment, next to the gas heater, her legs crossed, looking at her books and being quiet as if listening to the rustling of the pines. "It was his ambition. I mean, in order to make money, he started performing abortions and, as you can imagine, he did them on the kitchen table which then became an operating table in the grand style—a far cry from the little scissors and little knives and spoons of the little toads and frogs—with a complete set of surgical instruments, a clinical notebook and a white apron. He carried his money to the bank in sacks. That was what did it. Not frigidity."

She waited for my opinion. I said nothing. I just looked at her. There was sincere devotion in the way we lied to each other. We knew we had to talk because it was impossible not to. If we hadn't talked, she would have slashed her wrists, and I would

have caught the blood in a big washtub.
 We settled on the fact that it wasn't frigidity but his ambition. That's what we decided.

The Electric Chair

Sunday afternoon we went underground to see the Jewish couple.

People were weeping, hugging each other, throwing up their hands, demanding justice. They had kneeled down on a sandy surface pounded flat by the wind. Projected on a wall behind them was the bay.

At the base of the cliffs some dirty little waves were crashing, their foam flowing up between serious Japanese gentlemen sitting on the rocks fishing.

The sea was spread out at these gentlemen's feet, growing thicker and blacker toward the Farallons, then getting rougher and colder, covered with what looked like bits of glass and metal and stretching in every direction until it seemed to be an animal seizing the city with its claws, demanding, gnawing, with its fur flapping and its jaws snapping. Further out was a blur, soft gray edges, underwater reefs and nets hanging down from rainbows appearing and disappearing.

The people are crying softly now. There's some pushing and shoving among the new arrivals, and without even noticing the peaceful bitterness of these laments, they bump against the barbed wire. From a tower a uniformed guard shouts commands, tells them to go back home. But more people arrive. They get there and they kneel. Or they walk around in circles carrying signs with angry slogans. Housewives, professors, lawyers, students and children with glasses, little doctors of law, tiny old beardless men.

"What time is it?" someone asks, and a sharp howl goes up against the sheet of projected light which is the bay. The crucifixion must have been like this, a sky of obscene colors, an air of summer, a golden mountain and three men bleeding. But this isn't quite like that. The sky isn't over us but facing us, reflecting our unreality, the glow of humanity at its best, transcending the sea and its mirages as seen by an unmoved world which lets time keep spilling and sirens screaming and boats burning and prisons rotting, and here's where we get confused because it's a mirror where we can't even see ourselves and yet we find ourselves facing it, yelling.

Then a charge of electricity kills all the lights and we let out a scream, and then another jolt of juice and several more and our screams turn to a wailing, a prolonged lamentation, unstoppable sobs.

The little Jewish lady took several jolts before dying. She had a round head with curly hair. She asked about her little boys and tried to smile but couldn't. They'd shaved part of her head and strapped her securely to the leather seat so the generals could give it to her good and the President could slam another jolt into her and the senators could take turns shooting stronger and stronger blasts of electricity into her until smoke came out of her curls and the lady turned purple, beige, brown, and then was gone.

Then came her husband's turn and it didn't take so many jolts, even though his glasses were knocked off.

We cried all afternoon and didn't care what anybody said. They called us jerks and cowards: "They're killing the Jews in New York and here you are on your knees like fools." But we knelt and wept on the afternoon of the crucifixion, wept for the couple crucified and for ourselves, wept in bars, in bedrooms, without really knowing why.

My wife and I walked back from the execution without a word, crossing the beautiful golden red bridge which vibrated musically under high clouds, the sky was blue and the sea gulls dived and the radios played their sweet little songs and the ground kept burning, turning into something like a gorgeous multicolored tiger, and gently waves of people poured over it passing across the century, and suddenly night fell—a strange, open night—and we were torn apart when the first shock came, and it lit us up for an instant and we felt something like a blush rush to our faces, a silent sign of our humanity: man as criminal, man as beast, and also man in his solitude, grimacing man, man in his executioner mask and man in his saint mask, and in the hands we held, my wife and I, that too was man.

The Perfect Crime

Tahura had decided to get married and I decided to intefere. We were two people with a secret history which deeply intrigued those in the know: our faces bore the scars and marks of other lovers' abuses. We shared a passionate heroism, wise and sad, quiet and tired, dangerously violent and beautiful but defeated.

We'd teamed up for mutual support, with a certain disdainful skepticism but knowing it would be impossible—well, almost impossible—for us to betray each other. The fact that we'd end up betraying each other was somehow what gave us the strength to go on. I remember our first meeting was almost absurdly hostile. I thought she was a lesbian. I figured some teacher had taught her to look at men with contempt, if not revulsion, and that the black clothes and boots she wore now were sort of a suit of armor. I found out she lived with a wacky old woman, a seamstress who was always selling things and was rumored to be losing her marbles. Other women fought among themselves for the right to join the conspiracy and enjoy Tahura. On the other hand, men would drink with Tahura, enjoying the toughness of her company; they made eyes at her, tried to sneak in the window and seduce her, but she knew they were cowards and threw them out. Pathetic bastards. None of them had the balls to handle Tahura.

One night there was a party at Cuzco's place. When I use the word *party*, I mean to say a murder. It's one thing to come into a house and take the family out of the oven and go to the medicine chest and swallow a bottle of artificial kisses, and stab the walls with some popular songs and do a little dance as we give everyone their enemas. This kind of party—like our Easter services and deaths and births and baptisms, our confirmations and marriages and other respectable celebrations—will naturally take on a lively tone. But it's something else to come into my house, where the walls have been washed to hide the blood and there are suspicious hairs in the rug and the kitchen smells like the gas was left on all night and the window isn't a window but a mirror and the neighborhood is full of neon signs and barracks and vigilantes and there are towels on the table and toothbrushes and combs and deodorants as well as forks and plates and spoons and glasses and the vacuum cleaner, all warning you that you've entered a zone that nobody leaves except by force, screaming, drugged and dragged away by cops and paramedics who don't mind the party but can't stand the scandal we stir up just for the sake of dying in style.

Anyway, Tahura came to this party; she had on a silver dress and showed off her tits as she passed the drinks. Her cheeks were pink and her eyes were glassy and her face twitched a little to the sound of the traffic on the nearby freeway. Out of the basement rose a sound like rats racing over sand. I asked her which one was her boyfriend and she showed me. A bicycle mechanic with a gold tooth. He struck me as a rather sad person.

He grinned and his mouth gleamed. I liked his big, ironic, bloodshot eyes; they seemed to say that his engagement to Tahura was a game she dreamed up to remind her of her country, where couples really get married and before the wedding reveal to each other exactly what they're ashamed of and accept each other at the level of survivors who agree to stick together. The mechanic was picking his teeth with an ivory toothpick. I took Tahura into a corner and, drinking my wine with one hand and copping a feel with the other, offered my opinion. I told her the marriage would never work, that his kind of person didn't exist where we came from, that he'd bury her under a pile of dirty clothes and dirty dishes and television programs and phony friends, and that someday he'd probably kill her by smashing a bottle over her head. I piled on the reasons, from various viewpoints, but always emphasizing two things: the weight of that gold tooth and the danger of a violent death I could see already like a brand stamped on Tahura's naked back.

"This mechanic," I said, "with his little moustache and his silk handkerchief, has no intention of marrying you. He's putting you on. He likes the engagement party, he likes the ceremony, he likes the rice and the exchange of rings, he likes the honeymoon at the beach, he likes to lean over counters in delicatessens, he likes all that stuff but he'll never be married to you, look at his little mustache and his sad eyes, he's going to spend all his money on body work, he'll be scared to death when he sees you in the morning without your makeup. I'm telling you, you'll never be married to this guy. Not what you call married."

Tahura was convinced and broke the engagement. From the start it was clear to us there was no way I was going to replace the mechanic. With that understood, Tahura moved to another floor where it was quieter and there was a window looking out on the Masonic temple. I began to spend all my afternoons there while she went to work at her seamstress job. I waited for her to come home so I could kiss her and help her off with her clothes like I thought it ought to be done. Let me explain. The living room was small, barely big enough for a sofa, and on that sofa Tahura barely fit and, together, we just didn't fit. Well, I helped her undress. Tall, big, strong, powerful, Tahura had a mouth that was softly sad, but when she stood up she was like some beautiful gladiator out of the past, with broad shoulders, long legs and sinewy brown thighs. In front of the mirror she'd slowy sway as she climbed on top of me, covering me completely with her writhing hips, pounding, pumping, emptying and filling until she came, collapsing on me with her hair in her eyes and her mouth open. The oceanic power of this woman washed over me, splashing like coppery sunlight on the afternoon windows, black hair flying, the city breathing, her naked neck sweating and the orgasm building, thickening, moistening and spilling and the smell filling the room.

Later she gave me a cup of tea and tried to turn me on with a sheer black nightie. I broke out in a cold sweat, looked out the window trembling and noticed a black car parked on the street with its doors open, the cypress and eucalyptus trees in the distance. I was starting to feel the hollow where my body should have been on my own bed beside the sleeping body of the wife I loved so much. I drank the tea out of the saucer, saying yes, go ahead, as she went down on me, nibbling and licking. Then, I swear to God, I zipped up and got out of there. I didn't even save her from the mechanic, I didn't help her get her life together, I didn't protect her from anything. As a matter of fact, I had a damn good time getting her into all kinds of messes. It was the perfect crime.

Spontaneous Generation

Then came another couple. I was going down to ask for bread when they went by with their suitcases and we said hello. She was dressed in blue, looking very pale, and wouldn't look me in the eyes. He was short and dark, he blushed and tried to smile at me with his eyes but they clouded over, even though he kept looking at me as his face darkened.

Time Payment

At eight in the morning I had an interview with the Director. To get to his office up on one of the top floors, I had to go through three of his aides. The first—that is, the third in rank—is the only one that counts: a tall, heavyset, darkish man who speaks a strange language, wears a tattered toga and shepherd's boots, spits when he talks and carries a sidearm. This man hated me at first glance and decided to shut every door in my face. Translated, what he said was: "Have a seat. The answer is no." I asked him about his health and his wife's. He answered that everything must be done strictly according to the letter of the law. I wondered aloud about the spirit of the law.

"In this house," he said, "there is an order and a hierarchy, including a prejudice against the likes of you. This tradition must be maintained, *will* be maintained. Things will improve for you if you'll just be good enough to submit, screw yourself into your chair, keep your watch on, leave the door to the toilet open so you can be seen at all times, smile when you're spoken to, buy life insurance and drink lots of ice water. I can't guarantee it, but things could change."

"This place doesn't scare me, sir, and since I've got no place to go I'm at your service."

"How many years have you been here?"

I blushed and said I didn't know.

"I'll tell you," he said. "You arrived here skinny and stubborn, with a little mustache; you were aggressive, ignorant and visionary, and a liar besides. You tricked us, you robbed us. You got fat and lost your backbone, a lot of your hair fell out, you have a calculated grin between your wrinkles, you're an average dancer, your nose is longer and you've begun to look like an Indian. I'd say that if you ask the Director to release you he'll say no. Ah, but he'll see how old you are. Could be he'll invite you to lunch," he said smiling and his little eyes gleamed behind his glasses and on his bald spot the antenna spun happily. "In this war, my friend, I've had prisoners like you before, soft little people who practically begged me to take them out on the patio every day before eating and make them kneel down while I stuck the barrel of my gun in the back of their neck. While they twitched and trembled I wound my watch. So don't give me any of your bullshit. You can go into the Subdirector's office now."

I counted the cash in my pocket, taking stock. I'm buying two children, a house, a table and four chairs on time; I'm buying a little water, a little gas (to have on hand, just in case, for suicide), I'm making a weekly payment in blood pressure, I'm renting a meatgrinder and part of a refrigerator where other families can keep their leftovers.

Then I went in to see the Subdirector. Ready for anything.

The Mysterious Photo

The newly arrived husband came to see me. His name was Cuzco.

I invited him in. We both felt a little uncomfortable but were very courteous, gentlemanly. I sat down in an armchair and put my feet up on a footstool. I sensed that something was bothering him, then I sensed something like an inner grin. I liked him. No doubt he noticed the holes in my shoes. But why was he blushing so much? I wondered how old he was. I offered him a glass of wine and he accepted.

I noticed his hands were no bigger than a little girl's and just as chubby, a deep brown, almost black. I liked this new husband who showed up so mysteriously. Besides, he was so little and round and black: black hair, soft black eyes, black turtleneck (a little short, leaving a bit of his black belly showing), baggy black pants, short legs and little tiny feet like Madame Butterfly. And he spoke with a strange accent.

We really didn't know what to talk about. So we kept quiet and as we looked at each other, he blushed. He took a book out of his pocket and handed it to me. "Do you want to see it?" he asked.

"Yes, of course," I answered and began leafing through it. It was some kind of an essay on the cinema. As I turned the pages, a photo fell out. Picking it up I shot him a quick glance and handed it back. His eyes were moist and gentle, very large, like an Andean llama's. He stammered something, his tone was very respectful. Seeing I hadn't understood, he repeated what he'd said.

"Go ahead and look," he said, "it's for you to see."

I took the photo in my hand and examined it carefully. It was a badly taken snapshot of a naked couple fucking. The woman was very white, a blonde, with her legs way up in the air and a tremendously pained look on her face, and the man was a huge black whose smooth thick back looked like the barrel of a piece of heavy artillery.

"I took it myself," he said.

"It's beautiful, Cuzco. Do you have more?"

"No, not right now. Maybe later."

He got up gracefully. I noticed he had on sandals.

"You can keep the book," he said, "I'll come for it later."

I wanted to keep the photo too, but I didn't dare say so. Sensing my indecision, he added: "The picture is yours. Do you like it?"

"It's very lovely."

He smiled, blushing, and shook my hand. "Thank you for the wine. I'll be back. I mean, I'll come with my wife if that's all right."

"Of course. It will be our pleasure."

You couldn't hear his feet on the stairs as he left, just a catlike padding.

It had gotten dark. In some window the dirty streetlamps of Telegraph Avenue would be on and above them, like a theater curtain, a hillside covered with little lit-up houses. A kind of nativity scene. In my room I was in the dark with the picture in my hand and the book in my lap.

The City Plan

I left our flat, walked quite a ways down the hall—let's say several blocks—and then took a sharp right. There I faced an even longer hall, the same color, sort of pinkish, the floor and ceiling a bloody beige, with the same opaque lightbulbs every twenty paces, same doors, with the numbers on tin plaques. I didn't meet anyone, didn't hear a soul. I took another right, thinking I could begin to come full circle, but this hall dead-ended at a zinc door. I didn't want to go back the way I'd come so I opened the door and started down a cement staircase. As I went down, I noticed that on the other floors the hallways split off in all directions and that, on some levels, the stairways turned into gently sloping ramps. There were no windows anywhere. The light from the bulbs was identical, solid, authoritarian. Yet there were no guards or custodians. Like I said, I saw no one and heard nothing.

Thinking my stroll was getting a little long and that I should be heading back to my apartment, I concluded that this house we were living in was bigger than it looked and that there must have existed a master plan in some government office. The problem, in any case, was a matter of getting back to my flat, not of discovering the plan. So I earnestly set about solving that problem.

Dancing and the First Fire

Then Cuzco took his wife, Judith, by the hand and led her from the kitchen into the living room. Both of them were smiling with the childlike purity of schoolkids playing ring-around-the-rosy. My wife and I were smiling too, she sitting very dignified in her wicker chair—erect and remote but kindly, her white hair framing her forehead, her mouth firm but with a certain softness-and I lying on Cuzco and Judith's bed, hands behind my head, smoking and watching.

We'd just eaten some little black animals, hard and juicy, which Cuzco had caught at the garbage dump on the Emeryville beach flats. Judith prepared them with garlic and parsley and basted them with butter. They looked like wood ticks but they weren't insects exactly; someone might have taken them for spiders. But that would be absurd: they didn't have legs like spiders and they didn't move as fast and they didn't spin webs. They were slow and fat, with only four feet, feet which Judith adored and stuffed especially with rum and rice for after dinner. They had just one eye on top of their tiny heads and a teensy-weensy yellow slit on their chests from which it was possible—and we did it, being among friends—to suck out a thick, intoxicating marrow, like blood whipped up with some violent brandy.

That's why we were smiling. Because the animals had—no doubt about it—an obvious sense of the happiest friendship.

Cuzco and Judith, holding hands, barefoot, she dressed in red and extremely white-skinned, he with a blue shirt and green corduroy pants, walked in a circle, starting a certain Andean dance whose purpose they never explained to my satisfaction. The style of leading was French; the manner of advancing, Spanish, heel-clattering, upright with shouts; and the retreat was, well, sheepish, in the manner of sheep anticipating the prick of a horny ram. All the while their smiles were angelic.

On the floor, a red brick floor, there was a record player and the music sounded like an Algerian march against De Gaulle. One got a sense of the Algerians' courage marching through a sandstorm with their lances raised, charging ahead to a furious drumbeat.

Cuzco led Judith into a corner, turned out the lights and went to sit at my wife's feet. She looked at him distractedly, then with a more direct tenderness, stroking his black hair ever so gently.

We stayed that way quite a while: motionless in the whitewashed room whose walls and ceiling seemed to retreat into a kind of Castilian plain, slowly sipping our imitation rum. Judith was standing on a burlap rug spread all the way out to the patio; I was lying down on the bed; the purple rhododendrons were boldly thrusting their round flaming heads through the window; and my wife was quiet, introspective, wise and gray in her chair which gradually began to spin as the night darkened, building to a dizzying speed.

From the kitchen came a warm smell of onions, garlic, peppers, fresh bread, and along the floor ran a cool purple wine feeling for our bare feet. Cuzco was sobbing and smiling like a little boy. Judith was naked in her corner and in her right hand she had a gold flashlight which she shone sweeping over different parts of her body as if kindling a fire. We could tell that peace was beginning.

The Saint of the Library

I got up and said: "I'm going to the library."

Two things were on my mind: a death that was going to occur there that night and the cup of tea I was going to have at Tahura's, one fragrant cup with her big long naked legs.

I entered the library by way of the underground. A woman showed me the way. Her purple pants clung tightly to her ass. I crossed the reading room and noticed something in there was entertaining the crowd; their heads—and it was a colorful group—were shaking with laughter. Some climbed up on the tables to see better and raised their arms, pointing to the ceiling. The young ones threw down their notebooks and pencils, yelled at each other, shoved one another around and cracked up laughing. The racket distracted me too and I started wandering around looking up at the glass floor. This glass wasn't so thick that you couldn't make out the subterranean maneuvers of the librarians above. Only the couples looked deformed by the light and the cut of the glass. For example, a wide thick shadow, with white shoes and no head, withstood the attack of a gray smear in a cordovan hat that was wetting its pants. There must have been a chair between them because, the whole length of the corridor and all the way down the bookshelves, four steel paws and a cashmere seat were multiplied to infinity.

The reason for the excitement was simple: in the plaster vault, lit by the night's reflection, its dome painted with archangels, flags, sparrows, arrows and zithers stuck to the ceiling, a pane of glass had broken and through the hole came some fat pigeons, blue ones, which were chasing each other around and attacking one another in a flurry of wings and drizzling blood, blood that fell on books, heads and shirts creating a summery atmosphere. But that wasn't all. The pigeons flew way up in the nave of the library and slipped out through the opposite end where a crack had opened letting in thick clouds of fog.

Then an elderly reader, well known to everyone but who here will remain anonymous—a little old man of at least eighty, dressed in shiny black, with long thin blondish hair and a nicotine-stained beard and bloodshot eyes from trachoma, a little old guy, I tell you, whose spine had bent in two, obliging him to walk at right angles close to the floor, and whose good luck had provided him with an inheritance on the condition that he stay a professional student and who, on account of this, had quite a few bachelor's degrees and doctorates—jumped up, took his books, stormed past me cursing the pigeons, went up the marble stairs to the first floor, looked for the toilet, left his books on the floor, entered the stall, pulled down his pants, sat down and dropped dead.

They couldn't move him because of the rigor mortis and the right angle of his spinal column and the narrow marble walls of the toilet stall.

But the library building itself was a monument donated by Hearst the Father, god of paper, whose tumultuous and mysterious life turned his death into mountains of lead, concrete platforms, phallic towers, schools for deafmutes, venerable museums and crematoria, so there was no problem turning this old guy into a plaster monument to Rage and dedicating this wing of the building to his memory.

Because such a thing fit fine in the tradition of the house, in the rah-rah spirit of the graduates and in the fraternity's devotion to the esoteric. Such that the first floor of the northeast wing of this house was, from then on, a pilgrimage spot and the pilgrims started coming in sweaters, jeans and white shoes to pray to him several times a year and write him messages on the walls and floor and leave relics, especially before finals and football games.

The young ones were especially devoted to him and at night they stuck their heads out the window and, clutching their bellies, yelled in their fattest voices: "Peter! Peter! Peter!"—which was the old man's name.

The saint's grotto was like this: you got there through the corridor; in the middle of the room, separate from the other cubicles, was the figure, sitting on the pot, with his plaster pants down, his books, also plaster, on the floor, his shirt tails hanging out, his hands on his knees, torso leaning forward, stiff white head facing infinity (actually the wall in front of him), everything, as I said, in yellow plaster, except his ears, symbol of understanding, which were marble; behind him, a block of Arizona granite in which these words were engraved: *Mens sana in corpore sano*, and below that a brain held in the hands of a baseball player dressed in red-white-and-blue; on either side of this sphynx there was a niche: in the right one, an Amazon trying on a girdle and, above her, the face of her husband saying: *It's not whether you win or lose, it's how you play the game*; in the left, a pathologist peering through his microscope and, on top of his head, wrapped in a white halo, a madonna with big breasts pouring out milk, saying: *Milk has something for every body*.

As in any sanctuary the pilgrims leave their crutches, their wooden legs, glass eyes, corsets and false teeth as a sign of penitence or a token of thanks, so these students deposited at the old man's feet or on his lap or his shoulders, or in the niches, their relics: the competitive boyfriend left some nylon stockings; the faithful wife, her pill; the flat-chested girl, her falsies; the bearded woman, her Gillette; the fat lady, her tires; the speed freak, his uppers; the sleeper, his opium; the horny one, his peyote; and the eunuch, his resignation.

The old guy looked like a Turkish bazaar on his toilet: they hung earrings on him, they put on rings, shoes, scarves, pins, they wrote on his forehead, his chest, his legs and his back; they burned incense, surrounded him with candles, dressed him in black, in red, in green, in purple; they sang to him and played the flute for him.

The pilgrimmage to his shrine kept on continuously. And the old man began to work miracles.

Summer Solstice

Meanwhile the rains and the frost on the orange groves of Soledad and Gonzales were ending, and on the other side of the hills, above the solitary blimp advertising Cinzano, the scream of the afternoon strung itself out: a single wave of happy voices and tired airplanes, of hot and sweaty trains and tow trucks, sifters and silos where lovers fell silently, dreamily rolling in the hay. I wandered off across the countryside, following the road of the rose bushes. A myrrh tree like a Chinese lantern threw its yellow fuzz over my head. In my hand I carried our old silver key. Veronica had told me Rosamel was working that afternoon. So I waited, hidden among the trees. I saw him come out with a scarf around his neck, bareheaded, numb-looking, and lose himself in the crowd. I had a month stored up, a hard stiff month, bursting with juice. I opened the door. The white poodle started barking and when I came in it jumped me, knocked me onto the couch and started licking me like crazy. Veronica, standing there breathless, tried to pull it off. We turned out all the lights but one. We sat down in Rosamel's easy chair. She handed me a bottle of cognac and took out her Italian records. Then she threw herself at my feet. Her shoulders were bare, her dress rolled up above her thighs. She started fighting with the poodle: she pushed it with her head, got it out of the way and began licking me hard and fast with the tip of her tongue; the dog attacked wagging its tail in her face. Veronica kept her eyes half-shut and her mouth open; then the dog barked, loud. Veronica barked too, held the dog between her legs and took control of my lap, caressing me, covering me with kisses. She'd left a little light burning by the garden balcony. With my jacket on but naked from the waist down, I lifted Veronica gently, as one would lift a nylon building, and set her on top of me. And with the dog jumping all over her and pushing her from behind, Veronica started shaking her hips and I saw her tits in my face, and her thick calves, her black high heels, and I stretched to get inside her. The tower rubbed, grew, got hard, got in, filled up like one white arm of hers and mine, and the bells began ringing and the jasmines blooming and the fig trees dripping and I gave out a moan and lost my breath and began to fall and Veronica moaned too, and at the window, next to the only light, with his scarf, bareheaded, numb-looking, there was Rosamel, watching.

State of Siege

It was the start of a cloak and dagger adventure. Rosamel, totally bald, made it look like he wanted to shatter the serenity of the place: he spoke of divorce. He adjusted his glasses, stroked his silky little mustache and cleared his throat. But more than just his words, what caught my attention were his blue Eisenhower jacket and burgundy cords. The truth was, he already belonged to a group of lightweight low-grade philosophers who did their thing in the caves of Russian Hill. That's where the bottled Hungarians showed up, the whites from the Rhine, Yugoslavian violets, sparkling Italians dancing in huge men-only fiestas to the sound of balalaikas, mandolins and accordions. But we—Veronica, the poodle and me—knew that Rosamel was going through a bad time, that he was boiling with jealousy, that he went away out of pure spite, and that he could come back any minute and kill us. His problem was simple: rage had made him hysterically impotent. While Veronica kept spreading below the waist, brimming with a brown lava that ran down her thighs and over her knees and caught me in its current and swamped me, the poodle climbed on our heads and the three of us shut ourselves up in the dark in a padlocked loft. Suddenly Rosamel appeared. I jumped out the window and he froze, listening. I drove into the hills on my chopper and, looking back, could make out Rosamel with his scarf fluttering, his eyes glued to my back, sizing me up for the final stroke of his blade.

So Rosamel started standing guard. And weeks went by when I couldn't see Veronica. One afternoon the sentinel fell asleep. Veronica climbed on my bike and we split to score some pills. When we got back to the house, Veronica asked me to help her off with her clothes. Something's up, I thought, the tricky bitch. In fact, her dress was leather and, dropping, didn't drop all the way off because it got hung up on a very find sheer fishnet bodystocking wrapped around her from throat to feet, and I couldn't find a single button on it, or a clasp or a zipper, nothing. It was like a birthday suit. All of a sudden, playing, she turned around and—amazing—I found the secret: there were an infinite number of little knots which, as you undid them, unpeeled the net, and her waist and ass appeared in the darkness. As I finished my explorations and stepped out of the room, there was the sentinel waiting for me: he put the point of his sword to my throat.

"In here," he said, pointing to the greenhouse.

"Where? What?"

He clapped his hands. Veronica's beautiful bungalow never seemed so magical to me. The loquats opened up outside, mandarin oranges rolled down the hills, camellias spun silently like little propellers. Rosamel had gotten his buddies together. They were burning incense. I looked for a glass. They weren't drinking. I didn't like their silk and leather outfits either. Rosamel was looking me over, flashing me a sneer with his little rice teeth. In the fireplace they were roasting some little animal on a spit, the smoke was nauseatingly sweet and curly white hairs were burning on the coals. It was some kind of ritual, not a meal. For the initiates, on the other side of the house a chorus of voices and electronic instruments were repeating a single phrase, beating out the rhythm so violently the lightbulbs bounced. Rosamel led me back to the bedroom. On the bed, on the vicuna coverlet, he had Veronica tied down. "Sing," he said to her. And to me: "Dance."

I started dancing with a passionate concentration, trying to be as graceful and deliberate as possible with every step and every movement of my hands, scarcely moving my head and indicating with my shoulders that I could feel the weight of the whole world. The others watched me and didn't say a word. Rosamel, mounted on Veronica, was going at it, riding her with a tight rein down narrow paths and sudden drops, bounding along toward broader panoramas. I climbed on Rosamel and joined the exodus, rummaging in my pockets for a match, feeling the night was swallowing us and that soon the cold would be unbearable. Then the sons-of-bitches jumped me. The whole gang really let me have it. They said, "Fly," and beat harder, falling on me from the shelves and closets, breaking glasses over my head, flicking me with dogtail whips. Veronica was moaning. Rosamel was whispering something in her ear. The bash lasted till past midnight.

Outside, later, it was a truly enchanting night: little cars were going by on the avenue leaving a river of beer cans behind them, the movies were letting out, the windows of the little restaurants were steaming with their smell of grilled meat; a truck went by spewing thick streams of water. The gardens were calm, so peaceful, and their multicolored lights were reflecting up out of the puddles. Veronica walked behind me not saying anything, full of a relaxed happiness just like mine, a sort of presentiment of all the nights, so many years, when we'd walk like this, just like this, filled with love and empty at the same time, seasoned veterans of a local war, taking deep breaths, looking around, one step after another, on the way back home.

Summer created its own light, a light the wind wouldn't leave alone; we traced its changes from the house in the hills to the white towers and from there to the streets and the pier, over the pine trees to the open sea, shining, burned by an invisible sun. The copper braziers were late coming on. The bottles were emptied fast and then served as lamps. The kitchens no longer had the ochre color of lentils but rather the seductive smell of seafood.

Veronica loved me in her way: she danced with me on a footstool. Rosamel walked around in the living room. Dancing, Veronica shook her arms full of watches and jingling coins; she leaped and hung herself up by the hair. I followed her along the floor, bent over, panting, weighed down with indiscretion. We had no future. "I'm really going to miss you," she'd said when we met. Her accent intrigued me, her z's and j's and exclamations; her charge of good health was magnetic, not to mention her energy jumping into bed. "Wait for me," she said, walking away with a towel around her hips; she took a quick shower and came out wet, suntanned, glistening, serious. She knew what she wanted and she had the moves, she pulled me on top of her, wrapped her legs around mine and, digging in with her heels and her waist going like a piston, shook me at an incredible speed, slapping me against her like someone lashing herself with a shark, making a shipwreck-like noise that rattled the chairs, the windows and the doors and had the neighbors upstairs and on both sides yelling for us to quiet down. Then she proceeded to get to know me better by gently kissing my face, my chest, my hands. At dusk she cooked me brown rice with mussel juice. Sitting in Rosamel's chair, I drank my chilled white wine and listened to her songs. And I came to a few conclusions.

Veronica's problem was a very bitter woman she had inside. She kept her at another level, locked up, deep in the interior of the strong woman she was. That's why she seemed a little rigid, uptight, because she was very set in her ways, with broad shoulders, a long neck, big hips, hard legs, and inside the flesh and bones was the one who cried, got scared, was tender with me, who gave out little cries in the night and was looking in me for another man, who wasn't me. I tried to convince her. "Look," I said, "touch this face, these teeth and these eyes, this nose, this belly, sink your hand in this grave of hair, dig in, make me scream. Trust me. There's nothing to lose. I don't know if I can learn to live with you, but we'll work it out in bed. Our nights will be happy. The days will be something else. I'm jealous, insecure, envious, weak, vindictive."

"I can't take this," the one inside said finally. I could barely hear her voice. I got up during the night: I whispered things in her ear, to see if the one inside would speak and catch Veronica in some lie. I went out without a sound and walked along the lake shore; I walked down the sand paths taking the park in, measuring the distance between the lamp posts, from a red sign to a blue one, gritting my teeth, raging mad, thinking about her, how she used to walk here in a big straw hat and a flowered dress. Then she woke up and felt the bed and saw that I'd gone and heard the screams of people getting mugged in the night. At dawn I found an open window, climbed in, took off my pants, went upstairs, walked into the bedroom, stripped naked in no particular hurry, got in bed and pulled the covers up over my eyes. I slept snug and happy next to my old pals in my straitjacket.

Veronica heard me tell her to leave me in peace, that she was too much of a whore, that walking through the living room while she was doing her yoga with the neighbors annoyed me, that would she please go down on me, that with one I had a surplus but two Veronicas, the outside one and the inside one, well, they busted my balls. Until she couldn't take it anymore. She locked herself up in the inside one; she threw the key away, tossed it in the lake, walked off with the stride of a Salvation Army officer, taking my advice: she hated me. Sooner or later she'd marry Oblato; he was stronger than me and Rosamel, more of a man than either of us. But Oblato knew nothing about the other one: the one inside.

Funeral Pomp

My little wife appears in a transparent pink dress that makes her shine like a wet sponge. Then that slightly incredible interval occurs. Sitting down, not quite facing me, looking with a very natural attention at the naked wall, she says: "Here comes Lope."

In fact, Lope, who turned 76 today, comes bounding down the stairs yelling at the top of his lungs that he won't die. But he speaks too soon. Then my wife sets about describing a kind of life where we give in to everything, without any kind of boundaries, a good comical life, and Lope feels the tears welling up, his face twitching like those tics in a horse's flank, and he starts staring at us, trying to seduce us. Lope had come in dripping wet, with his necktie twisted and his white hair messed-up. In order to give him the shot to put him to sleep, four people hold him down and another sits on his face. Then they take him to his room and his friends look for his pajamas. Meanwhile, the doctor orders him transferred to a hospital. Lope's dying! Hard as they look, his friends can't find his pajamas. Lope sleeps in his swimtrunks. So they put them on him, lay him out on a stretcher and carry him to the elevator. But the stretcher doesn't fit in the elevator. His friends decide to take him down the stairs and he dies in his swimtrunks before they get to the first floor.

This kind of person is a pain in the ass. On the other hand, the type who lives a quiet life and is screaming inside and makes people believe it's openness and generosity that makes him stay with his family year after year winds up flipping out. Lope got bitter so as to die unobtrusively. Nevertheless, he died demanding attention. My wife wasn't interested in this line of reasoning. She had something else on her mind, she was looking beyond Lope, maybe I could figure it out. Without referring to herself she wanted to introduce me to someone or something connected somehow to her.

"I had a girlfriend," she said, "from a very wealthy family. When she was still quite young, she decided to marry an old man. The interesting thing is that she began putting distance between us with a strength, a wisdom and a maturity that were really remarkable. At 17 she could walk like an astronaut. She manipulated people in a brusque and precise manner. At 19 she slit her wrists with a pair of needlepoint pliers. And since suicides are usually evil and dangerous people, she did everything possible, everything humanly possible, to kill Lope."

"They're vicious schemers," I said.

"But I don't want to be unfair. The girl came back every now and then, just for Lope's sake. It was the right thing to do."

"It doesn't surprise me."

"Me neither. Besides, that's water under the bridge."

The Lovers

"I'm not making any demands," said my little wife.

And she wasn't. We were two survivors of a cataclysm, and now that we'd gathered up all that was left, we were scared to ask for more. That's how we felt, though we didn't say a word. We were afraid of losing everything.

But the woman and man who are afraid to lose turn lazy, with a tenderness always bordering on desperation, because sadness too is scary. That smile, the one I'm referring to, is always the same: it's fragile, and it disappears at the first premonition of a fall. The man and woman united by such a smile are like two glasses of water pouring back and forth: they fill up, they empty, but they never boil or smash because they've got nothing left to spill. And consequently they have amazing powers of intuition, observing each other's weakness, supporting each other like a couple of lovely invalids, helping each other along with their fingers, with their eyes and mirrors and medications, until one day they wake up terrified facing the reality of a terrible fatigue, and wrinkles like a stage curtain drop down their faces.

Anyway, we tried to set up a life for ourselves. Within the limits of what was possible. The music was soft, the singer a Brazilian sociologist named Gilberto who sounded like a kitten drinking milk out of a paper bag. We drank gin, which we stirred with our fingers. Our bed was covered with lion fur and a bestial dandruff. We kept a basin of holy water by the electric lamp. A vase of hideous paper flowers. And we ate like gourmet savages: big pots of seafood, octopus, oysters, eels, starfish and sand. Ferocious crabs, stuffed tomatoes, onions the size of industrial lightbulbs, big red and green peppers like swollen noses, huge cloves of garlic, chunks of flaming goat. We drank white wine from a sacred vineyard, crisp and cold as an icicle. Lying on the rug, we'd scratch each other, wagging our tails, licking each other like cats. And when we got older, mature and wise, we'd yell and throw our old clothes out the window like flags informing the neighbors of our pleasure. I went to bed with my hat on and she, understanding, picked up the habit and so, with our hats on—mine Andalusian, hers straw—we pounded the life out of each other. She was dark, her face covered with scars, you could barely see her eyes, it was overwhelming—to me, anyway—she was burying me and I banged with my feet until the gravestone toppled and we opened our eyes, amazed by the years, the light, and life itself, which was left in a puddle on the sheets like a watery mirror.

Then came a serious conversation: about money.

String Orchestra

The three of us began a violent romance. Violence is assumed when we've lost the notion of security implicit in sin. Let me explain. Cuzco came to my room dressed in black, now with a beautiful silk necktie which hung down his chest like a giant tongue; he sat down on the red floor at my feet scarcely taking up the space of a clay flowerpot, with his brown head and sweet eyes inside the pot, talking about his mother, his brothers, some girlfriends in the mountains who taught him to sew, and as we laughed and drank our rum, the hours passed and, every so often, he took my hand and held it between his cool little boneless hands and described to me the beginning of an episode that kept coming back in all his memories: in a shining valley, possibly paved with glass, at the foot of a capitalist mountain, the peasants of the country come together and beat the air with their revolutionary flags and picket signs. They've just instituted the land reform but they're not happy, they're furious, and their blackbeards are flapping in the wind and they're all yelling, but you can't make out what they're saying. Camera number 1 swoops down like an eagle off the mountain for closeups of the faces. There's a little blood. Then the Prince of the country appears. The revolutionaries run behind a very white church and Christ comes climbing down a barbwire chainlink fence, like a prison's. Gunshots. Buckshot. Then the shooting dies down. The Prince smiles, pleased, but suddenly the Prince and the peasants all lose their faces. It seems like instead of faces they now have mirrors and they look at each other but there's nothing there.

We crack up laughing because Cuzco wants to make a movie with Anthony Quinn and assures me that the peasants and the Prince could put on Anthony Quinn masks, so the revolution would be of man against himself, in himself, for himself. Then we make plans for the violence.

The violence begins when we accept it as punishment for the pleasure we give each other, or an evil that's ours which we can't deny, that is, the thread of love that runs through our palms and hangs us up, stuck front to back, like dogs.

Summing up. It's 10 in the morning. Cuzco sends me a mysterious message. I get it. I get dressed fast and go to his flat. In the blood-colored felt armchair, Cuzco is sitting with one leg up in the air. Next to him, on a little table, there's a tray with three martinis and some crackers; Judith is standing in a corner, her hair down over her face. She's white, but she looks as if she's bathed in honey, wearing a black bra and panties, black stockings, but her teeth are white, and she's barefoot. Cuzco taps his baton and we begin the return to the sweetness after the martinis. We're going across the California desert toward Arizona, the surfaces shimmer like a red belly, above the cactus and the sagebrush the sky astutely changes colors without giving anything away; on the contrary, always growing and wrapping us up and turning the world into an arid aquarium. Between the mountains, coming out of the rocks, what could be called a really dirty trick—a white church—stops us dead in our tracks. It's called La Paloma, The Dove. Cuzco keeps time with a kind of abandon. But we know he's not happy. We dance with greater concentration, but in no hurry. Judith has taken my clothes off like a tailor taking my measurements. The wind whips down on us wisely. There's a frog croaking in Cuzco's lap. In a corner, Judith and I are kissing, loaded with milky juice. Cuzco changes the beat. The baton flies. He makes me turn my back on him while Judith works me over with her long, nailless fingers. I've unhooked her bra and Cuzco makes her put it back on and asks her to take my baton in her hands and smile and sing its praises. We're in the wellhouse, from the depths of the well the icy green secret water bubbles up toward the volcanoes. The headless woman raises her legs in the air and makes them ring like bells. The spotted oxen approach to look and drink. Cuzco is furious and shaking his baton out of time. He's spread a vicuna pelt on the ground and, lying there, looks up at the stars. Judith and I are a gathering storm that keeps on building, allegro cantabile, the curtains flap, the doors bang in the wind, a teapot wistles. But now Judith is going around with a staff in her hand and is poking me in the ribs to see if she can draw water. It's a sweet and gentle rondo, full of words about her people and familiar questions loaded with a faith in the life of the chickens, the pigs, the cows, the dogs of her house, with a knowledge of milk, a longing for a fire where all the old things put away by her father and brothers in chests for her wedding day are burning. She's straddled me now and rides me with the rhythm of a marching band. She gets off and I can still see her violent full form in the air. She swept over me like a storm and soaked me with hot spurts. Now that we've drunk the martinis and I'm trembling flat on my face and searching in Judith for the key that would get me out of this, Cuzco, sitting in his armchair, implacably waves his baton and demands more, and his wife and I make him another shaker of martinis, this time with her watching my feet and me breathing into her back. I'm pouring flame into her kidneys and the juice falls drop by drop at my wrung-out feet. Then we talk about the war, about paratroopers and a film with mental retards, freaks and siamese twins. "Civilization is a worm in the belly of cannibals," says Cuzco, with which one can only agree, because the super people seem to like that belly and become attached to its intestinal flora and prefer the exit through the digestive tract to all the others. I want to say something but Cuzco won't let me. I beg for mercy. Cuzco frowns, demanding more and more. But I can't, I've got nothing left. Judith is on her feet, head cocked, smiling as she sings sweet songs and strokes me with both hands. A pity. I begin to distrust the little bridegroom I knew who was so respectful and devoted and dedicated to turning the guts of the world around with his baton, who now jumps yelling on Judith and digs in his spurs and whips her and rips the desert backdrop and drops big rocks in the well and drinks like a horse.

The martini fountain has dried up, so now I'll go back to my flat with a load—inside me, walking inside me—of Judith and her brothers and my whole family, and the pain isn't in my kidneys anymore but in my feet.

I'm quite a walker.

Head on a Plate

I loved Judith in a strange way. I waited for her calls, which never came. I knew that in some corner of the house she was enjoying herself under Cuzco's baton, the battery-driven electric one which vibrated, with little red lights on the tip that looked like me. But she never called. Nor Cuzco either. I missed his sweet look, his flute-like voice, the lower half of his body which sometimes glowed among my books, broken, like an Incan beer mug. I thought about his intuitive gifts and asked myself why, knowing my pains and anxieties, he closed the door, hid his wife, hung black drapes over the windows and still had me followed, paying his spies to take my picture. Judith appeared before me everywhere: on the dinner table, in the bathtub, in the oven, even in my clothes, and I always had her the same way. She started out with her tongue from bottom to top, from side to side, from top to bottom. First the flat of her tongue, then the tip. She stretched out between my thighs like she was made of olive oil and from her neck hung a tiny face the size of a penny, and I began to strangle her and her breasts got bigger and a beauty mark appeared in her armpit and out of her navel a dark face popped, not Cuzco's but mine turned into a knot like a necktie's, and her waist lost its shape and started dripping, all her vertebrae fell to the floor because I'd disarmed her and at one stroke rearmed her, but going all the way through her, trying to touch her nape from the inside, diving into her womb in search of the needle in the haystack, scratching her, tripping her, cutting off her legs and splitting them in two without losing count of each of her blond hairs and her moans, kissing her, licking her, whispering endless threats. She expressed her ecstasy like a sailboat rushing up onto a beach in sheets of foam. Her eyes fell out, she cried, she pounded the walls, and twisting like a spring she unwound in one leap crushing me between her legs, leaving me in the air while she flipped the tree of life over in her water, thinking to plant it there then pulling it out.

Cuzco took several positions. He didn't want to acknowledge my love for Judith. On the other hand, he was clearly aware of her love for me. Once we were sleeping in the biggest bed in the house and he stood at our feet, watching us without batting an eye, serious as a mirror. I turned my face and saw myself in Cuzco and saw Judith's tremendous body swimming desperately with no way out, coming and going from Cuzco's eyes to mine, banging into his forehead, coming out of me, returning to Cuzco's open arms which rejected her without touching her. Another time, he hid in the closet, climbed on a chair, wrapped a tie around his neck and, hearing Judith and me come in the door, took the big leap. The necktie broke. I stayed outside. And my watch stopped.

Not being able to see Judith, I left messages with her friends. It was a big mistake. Cuzco found out and tied her hands and feet together with a chain, which he then attached to her neck. I shouted to them from my flat. Finally they gave in. They came, but they ignored me and only spoke with my wife. When I said something they just kept eating, not even looking up. I was getting really mad. Then I lunged at my wife. Cuzco and Judith saw it coming, gritted their teeth and joined forces with her, offering to take my kids to their den while we fought. I slammed doors, smashed cups, threw plates on the floor and generally made a mess. Then everyone left. I spent the night passed out on the table. I woke at dawn with a terrible toothache and a tremendous depression which turned to terror. I spent the day spitting, making telephone calls. I ordered a crown for Cuzco and another for Judith. I hid from my wife. I spent weeks alone in my flat. Until my wife decided to forgive me and everything seemed to return to normal. But Cuzco was sharpening his machete, and Judith was cooking, sewing, ironing and singing, as if she'd never spread for anyone. This couldn't go on. And in fact it didn't.

One night the four of us were sitting at the table ready to eat. Judith went into the kitchen and a few minutes later I followed. Unzipping my pants, I stood in front of her and lied: I told her that Cuzco said it was okay. Even more. That Cuzco had ordered her to kiss my thing immediately and then go ahead with the whole thing, right away, however she wanted to do it. Cuzco's watching, I told her. She just laughed at me, she howled with laughter and started rubbing it with two spoons and shaking it with a feather duster, then she tried to wrap it up in a napkin. I slapped her, buttoned up as best I could and swore I'd get even.

We went on to the second course. Cuzco spoke of his childhood. He said that his parents had to travel to the capital and left him alone, him and his brothers, in charge of the house. The kids lived on whatever they could get at the town store; for weeks they ate nothing but candy, cake, cookies and soda pop. When the youngest got indigestion and another got scurvy and another tried to commit suicide, a telegram came announcing their parents' return. The twenty brothers decided to run away. Three got as far as California, where they're living now, two died crossing the river, one went to war, and fourteen, counting Cuzco, lived to tell the tale. I couldn't take it anymore. Using some lame excuse, I told Cuzco off. I called him a shit. He called me a traitor. We called each other faggots. That, instead of settling things down, threw us into a scuffle. I threw the snails in his face. He smashed a wine bottle against the wall. Judith hit me over the head with a loaf of bread. I tried to get closer to Cuzco, shoving things out of the way. My wife grabbed my arm and tried to stab me in the jugular with a fork. I shut my eyes and attacked, foaming at the mouth. I got tangled up in the tablecloth. I had a bead on Cuzco and lined up a knockout punch. But my sights were off and he caught me in the neck. I regained my balance. Cuzco was dancing. My wife hit the floor first, then Judith. I banged into a door. They turned on the gas. The lights went out. We ran yelling through the apartment. I couldn't find Cuzco anywhere. I kicked the stereo. Judith and my wife had me from behind and tried to tie up my hands with napkins. Cuzco, bobbing and weaving, kicked me in the shins. I was out of breath. Really tired, for Christ's sake. Why was I after Cuzco and not Judith? What was with my wife, how come she was pinching me so hard? I felt like having a cup of coffee but the coffee pot was on the floor and the coffee was dribbling down the walls. With my foot I pried apart some pieces of meat and found the bottle. The sun was coming up. The broken stereo kept playing a song that sounded beautiful to me, terribly beautiful. I got sad. Sobbing, I started to look for them to ask their forgiveness, to kiss their hands. I drank imagining the bottle to be a bugle in my hands and that I was supposed to blow reveille. So I blew, I blew along with Ray Charles who was the one singing "It's Crying Time" on the floor, in the corner, blind, with his ivory ribcage in his lap, and we both cried while Cuzco's chalk walls collapsed, crumbling on top of us and the moon came dripping through the cracks and dawn breathed through the window like a sick person and the leaves were left hanging alone in the green sky. Ray singing, and me playing the bottle. Maybe Cuzco was taking Judith for a ride. My wife was slumped on the closet floor, unconscious.

I decided to finish this once and for all. I walked through the darkness, turned on the light. I made a gesture toward Cuzco as if to strangle him. Judith was on her knees, weeping. Cuzco went running across the room and stopped near the beautiful machete I'd brought back from Guatemala. I froze, terrified. Cuzco was going to kill me with *my* machete. I tried to catch his eye, to reason with him, and he held my gaze. Then I realized that Cuzco wasn't with us anymore, that he'd died and was interested only in his transfer to the other world, in what was awaiting him there, in what it would cost to get there, in the aches and pains of the coffin and in his interview with God. The tears poured down my face and I felt that I missed him already and that I'd always love him and that someday I'd be sorry for throwing the snails in his face. Cuzco then took down the machete, unsheathed it, took a step forward, braced himself and brought it down with all his might on the back of Judith's neck.

The Greased Pole

This crime brought two results: first, my wife read about it in the papers and decided to come immediately; second, people started climbing all kinds of poles to see who could stay the highest longest, sticking their neck out looking down on their neighbors.

(At the time I was deeply worried about the country's destiny and spoke with friends and strangers, trying to come to some conclusion. I think the origins of the drama are in a kind of essential innocence, a beatific condition which is the product of a past full of slaves and workers who at some point in history find themselves sailing away aboard a ship. But sailing is not the same as arriving. To arrive and disembark one has to meet certain requirements. For example: you are not supposed to know how to read; you must have a concrete tent, nails, a hammer and a hatchet, a motorboat, fishing rod and gun; you have to swear obedience to one man; give your money to one woman; prefer the plains to the city and move continually from one plain to another; be able to build sheds with porcelain shelves to serve as markets, schools and cemeteries; know how to add, subtract and divide, but not to multiply; to ask your mother why she didn't take the pill; to surround the tent with decapitated geese.)

After several weeks of absurd stunts, the competition came down to a single test: sky-high poles were erected, on top of which was placed a platform with a metal chair, handles and a bucket. The contestants shimmied up the poles and stayed on top trying to break their rivals' record. Their food was brought up with pullies and their waste brought down in the bucket. There were some who stayed up for years. They made themselves at home, observing the world around them, waving at the light planes passing by, hunting birds by hand, forecasting the weather, getting old eventually, in harmony with the altitude, the rain, the sun, the moon and the stars. Searchlights beamed up at them from below and cars were sold in their name. This lasted as long as the memory of a crime but the time came when the novelty wore off. The lookouts came down, the lights went out and the poles were abandoned in the used car lots.

But one day the war escalated: helicopters dropped like flies; women with white blouses and black pants ran through the rice paddies with smoke pouring from their hair; the ground was covered with burning children; legless men fell on the generals' roofs; monks went up in flames; cities disappeared and in their place were craters and, in these, supermarkets were improvised and the dead laid out among the canned goods.

The same things happened at home: a president was assassinated; three youths were tied to a tree and whipped to death with chains; the Ku Klux Klan returned three eyes, and little pieces of brains to the relatives who claimed them; graverobbers started jumping from church towers and falling on passersby, ripping them open with knives, removing their organs and selling them for transplants. All of a sudden the killing process changed: instead of one person at a time, the butchers, dressed in blue with masks and shields, tear gas and electric cattle prods, went into the universities and, dragging them by the hair, smashing their faces against lamp posts or the ground, sticking billyclubs in their ribs, they began to kill people by generations, proclaiming a generation gap that had to be filled with blood, and it was filled, since the soda fountains invented a sangria which, instead of wine, used blacks as a basic ingredient, but when they got to the Chicanos—up until then a humble army, devoted, beaten but silent, the course of events was interrupted because a man yelling STOP got crucified on a greased pole.

Cuzco began to behave strangely. He ate in a corner, covering his plate with a piece of paper; sometimes he raised the paper like a screen, so we could see only his hair moving as he chewed and his belly bumping against the table. He hid in order to talk to himself, but he wasn't just hiding from us, he was hiding from himself too. He whispered out of the side of his face, staring at his hands and feet, rubbing his knees. He lost his furtive, catlike step and kicked off his sandals, and his body, which once had the lightness of a dark blimp, now moved slowly, sluggishly. What it came down to was that Cuzco was afraid that someone would get in his way; he avoided all bodily contact, he moved as if the slightest touch would set his skin on fire. But the fear was even more specific: he was afraid of being mugged. "You do the shopping," he said to me when Judith sent him to the market. He looked at me pleadingly but also with an icy indifference in his eyes.

"Why, Cuzco? Why don't you go yourself?"

His face sort of melted and gathered around his mouth. But his eyes didn't fool me: they were hard, cruel even. He never blushed anymore, never offered his dark little hand to shake. He walked alone down halls and sidewalks, hiding behind posts, his pants baggy as always, his black T-shirt sweaty. He didn't read anymore or collect pictures of his woman. They wouldn't serve him in restaurants; he'd sit down at a table and the waiters or waitresses would go right by, not even seeing him. He tried to call out but his voice was gone and all that came out were little whistling sounds. He couldn't even look straight ahead, so he'd trip over things. He started going out at night, all by himself. He got jumped a couple of times. He smelled strange, like a goat, a town square, a train station.

The situation became unbreatheable. Judith worked for both of them: in the morning she gave language classes, in the afternoon she posed nude on a bed so the students could take her picture, and at night she cooked for Cuzco, bathed him, put him in bed and sang him to sleep with lullabyes. Cuzco made impossible demands on her. "Bring home a black and an Indian," he told her, "take them to bed and let me fuck you from behind." Judith found a black or an Indian but not both at once. Then Cuzco would beat her up. She'd walk out, swearing she'd never come back. The next day we'd go out, Cuzco and I, to look for her and convince her it had all been a mistake. Cuzco would bring her some snails. They made peace, but not with me.

Then Cuzco stopped leaving the apartment. He lived in bed. Or rather, in a clump like a neutered cat, propped up on lots of pillows, writing poems and eating walnuts. At noon he'd take some martinis out from under the bed and drink till nightfall. Then Judith came home and he'd try to butter her and give it to her from behind like a prisoner of war. She'd moan and cry and finally come running to my flat.

"Cuzco, buddy," I'd say to him, "listen, don't get me wrong, for godsakes, but what you're doing to Judith is unspeakably cruel. And what's worse is the damage you're doing to yourself. It's a crime against nature, Cuzco. You can't go on like this, curled up in bed, hating the rest of the world. There are a lot of us who love you and we'd like the chance to help you."

I brought him martinis that day, and a cheese crawling with worms. Cuzco softened up. I was surprised to discover that in the past months in bed he'd weakened and his skin had changed color. His eyelids had disappeared and his face was just a shadow; his hair was sort of a vague stain. The skin on his ears trembled and he couldn't close his lips anymore. His tongue had turned purple. Besides that, you could say he had no legs, just a bust, a head and little hands. His fingers stuck to the martini glass and the worms from the cheese slithered up his arms toward the armpits.

His tenderness didn't last long. Suddenly I saw that he hated me. No. It was his wounded indifference, a visible eagerness to throw me out, to never see or hear from me again, to stay there alone with his worms, his martinis and his woman smeared with butter. I was going to appeal to his humanity but I kept my mouth shut. In his limestone room, behind his concrete door, Cuzco buried himself and kicked me out.

The neighbors heard their shouts and the banging on the floor. They could hear Judith praying, people fucking and groaning, the tea boiling and whistling, the insults of the police who refused to arrest anyone but came back night after night to turn off the lights, break his records and drink his martinis.

One Friday, after a whole night of screams, fist fights, curses, pleadings and prayers, Cuzco got dressed and made his getaway without Judith knowing he'd gone. He ran downstairs, from one floor to the next, till he reached the basement, climbed out a window, jumped the wall and, free, went trotting down the middle of the avenue howling. People looked at him, surprised. Some laughed, others yelled at him. After a few blocks, Cuzco had a pack of dogs on his tail. They didn't seem to want to catch him, just follow a few yards behind, within shotgun range. Cuzco had on his T-shirt but was naked from the waist down. You could tell he was worried about his behind and his skinny legs, but not too much, really; he'd placed his hands on his head and was sort of whimpering sadly to himself, his voice gone. He climbed a hill and soon was crawling and clawing his way along in order to keep a grip on the rocks and mud. Then the sun went down. I was stunned to see all these green faces in the night, lots of faces, faces I'd known all my life, hardened by the neon splendor emanating from within, faces with angry looks which had once encouraged me, loved me, pitied me. But they didn't notice me, they were watching Cuzco, who had climbed a greased pole and, from the top, stuck like a monkey on his metal chair, was yelling down unintelligible things.

That's how it went that Friday. The neon signs said FUCK THE SPICK. The crowd grew on Saturday. They didn't glow now, though. They were summer tourists in shirtsleeves, smiling, snapping pictures, eating hot dogs. The old ones made comments under their breath and shook their heads. The girls and boys shook the base of the pole yelling FUCK THE SPICK, FUCK THE SPICK. Cuzco stopped talking. He froze to the chair, his face to the sky, his eyes closed. From below they began to throw stones. The police lit him up with searchlights. Saturday night, a summer night, Cuzco looked like he'd been crucified, his head hanging, his little arms hairless, his belly in the air, half naked, one foot over the other, covering the nail hole. They turned more searchlights on him. He was criss-crossed with bands of light. The mob was furious, calling him chicken, begging him to jump, spitting and even shooting at him, waving flags and aiming firehoses.

The country's at war, I told myself, and offered Cuzco my hand. He returned the gesture, looking at me with terror in his eyes. Don't jump, I thought, tomorrow will come for sure and the sky will open, there'll be stars like always and breakfast will be by your bed and on the floor you'll see a pair of Judith's stockings, snapshots scattered around, and we'll link arms, little buddy, we'll drink our martinis like always, like every day, nothing will change, we'll hold each other, just you and me, and my wife will watch us tenderly, Judith will stand there undressing forever, maybe a little crazy or even kind of headless by now, and we'll come up next to the steaming pot and the sea will be inside and we'll drink and we'll dance. Cuzco, it will be another day, but the same day, together, just another day, locked up luke-warm in our house with its limestone walls, secure, loving each other as ever, forever.

Where There's Life There's Hope

So I was alone again, and my solitude was the worst kind, the kind you don't even notice but it has a smell and this smell starts climbing around sundown and filling us with a sort of steam so our bodies dissolve and then we can't breathe or pass the fluid filling our hands. Everywhere there are people sitting, reading, lighting cigarettes, losing their hair, and the sun is going down fast, not like a disc now but bloated and deformed like a drowned man. We don't say a word. I'm looking for my people. But they're not here. They've never been here. The ones who were waiting for me no longer know me. They'll say hello and invite me over to eat but you can tell they'd like to throw me out. Or that I just don't matter to them. Anxiously I search for reassurance but all there is around me are papers and ovens that burn everything. Everything but the bones forming a plate for gourmets with a half-baked pig's head, leather, thread and vegetables ready for the blender. I insist that I have a name, I have a metal tag on my wrist, fingerprints and teeth. This ought to help me find my family. I know they're around here somewhere. But when they see me and I speak to them, all they give me back is a distant smile. They don't even come to put flowers on me. And the others, the incredibly real ones, changed with the seasons and turned into others and these others have their own ovens and they have no right to bother us. I mean our roots get mixed up with the trees'. A big cedar grabbed me a while back and has me by the feet. Now that I've put out roots, I'm a tree. With one difference: we have faces. And we'll hide in boxes. And we'll defend ourselves tooth and nail.

Saint John the Baptist

I tiptoe into the bedroom; in the pink crib the child is sleeping face down with his little fists clenched. He's about the size of the Shepherd's hand who'd pick him up placing his thumb between his legs and pressing on his head with his fingertips. He has black hair and curly eyelashes and he seems not to be breathing, but he's still sucking with his milk-fed lips.

Outside are patriarchs, warriors, women with Mayan pitchers and vases from the Yucatan, young priests, poets, musicians and politicians, longhairs—some white, some black—with faraway peaceful expressions on their faces, slender, barechested except for their medals and amulets, all with long strong legs and cowboy boots. We drink in silence awaiting some revelation. Over the courtyard leafy vines are tangled in the fig trees' branches. Consequently, no one here is whole: I see a forehead or an eye, smiling lips, or a single arm or a crotch, or two tanned legs, or some sandals and buckles and some leather thongs; but no whole persons because at that hour of the afternoon the sun, the sky, the shade of the leaves, pick us up piecemeal and deal us out the same way.

In my wife's arms the child is a white bubble crowned with a black shadow. We lift the cup ceremoniously to our mouths, take cautious sips and approve. There's no music, no ballgames, no sacrifices. The priests run quietly down the paths hunting iguanas. From a gigantic willow the gathered animals watch the ritual on our terrace, motionless.

The silence and that stillness fill us with sweet thoughts. Somebody speaks of the ages passing in countries where there are nothing but leap years, of the old folks who one day in February get up and deck themselves out in ribbons and bells and dance on barrels of fermented honey and embrace falling in the mudpuddles made by the wine and fuck there happily; of the young who do the bellydance until their navels fill with pollen and then the tribal husbands prick them and oil and salt them, preparing for the wizards' nocturnal attack; of the children and the sheep, of adolescents and mares, peons and vicunas, of how the sun just stops one day and doesn't move, the people say nothing because it's dusk and a cool breeze comes up, and the calendars stop dropping their pages and it seems like a motionless springtime and suddenly a bell rings and we see that the clock's struck the month of February, and we look at each other and have a good laugh: the patriarchs, the priests, the warriors, the poets, the musicians and the politicians. Then the father pops a chamnpagne cork and the sun starts moving again with its customary tick tock and the foam shoots out spraying the vines and we drink to one another with a loud toast.

The mother has now taken the child in her arms and gives him her round pink freckled breast. Her blond hair brushes the child's face and all of a sudden he's the man who recognizes the age he's living in: with his wild black hair, his little nose buried in his mother's breast and his violet lips full of foam, sucking and licking. It's a little semicircle, like a scimitar, the blond mother and her African baby.

A gong sounds and Saint John the Baptist appears, tall, built solid, so black he looks blue, his nappy hair touching the vines;

he comes with his beard dripping with grapes and mango, wrapped in a red cape and carrying the child in his left hand, between his fingers, and he pours water from an earthenware plate on his head and with his rivery voice pronounces happy wise sentences on behalf of peace and the child. We raise our glasses, drinking now like delighted horses and shouting our toasts. The baby cries, the mother has bared both breasts and goes around giving us her milk mixed with champagne. My wife takes the lids off the pots and serves the red beans and rice and pigs feet and we eat in each other's arms, Saint John the Baptist and me, since I'm the godfather, trading affectionate little phrases. Saint John the Baptist then plays his gold cymbals, the sun goes down, the evening cools and it gets cold under the fig trees. The child has to be put to bed, covered and tucked in, sung to, and gently rocked to sleep while there is time.

The Hanged Man

I'll tell you simply what happened then, and this simplicity may sound a little strange on purpose. God knows I don't have any twisted intentions. I'm no pervert.

    I'm referring to Rosamel who, before being a philosophy teacher, took care of a clockman. I really began to get to know Rosamel after he died. That is, he began to open up to me and accept my intimacy freely. Before, he was the little sarcastic, officious, superior gentleman who put a past of twelve years between us like someone who crosses a river, burns the bridge and says laughing: "I got across." In those twelve years tons of water passed under the bridge. I don't deny it. But now he hid himself from me most astutely. Actually, he kept appearing to me like an eclipse: he showed part of those years obscured but you could see them, and hid three-quarters of his face behind clouds. The face I'm referring to was small, with green eyes when they weren't brown or coffee-colored, and a frowning mouth. "How you've grown!" he said to me. "You've become a man, a handsome man!" I held his joking gaze and asked him: "Are you perhaps Nicolai Andreyevich?" "The same." By now he was a mature man (I'll explain later where he was mature), very slender, with a large hard Adam's apple, something like an outcropping of rock, and he walked weakly, doubled over. I figured from the way he avoided me that previously a father-son relationship must have existed between us and that now this relationship wasn't understood. My back, my nose and my arms had grown, my eyes had a stubborn peacefulness and an obvious mistrust, both obstinate and implacable. My whole head had grown, in general, and he saw my face in two halves: the top half slightly tilted to the left, out of line, eyes included; the other fleshy, shameless, sort of naked.

Immediately we struck a gentleman's agreement, which he kept and I didn't. The obligation was to keep our shame under wraps and maintain a rigorous discipline of silent, pitiless criticism. This easily leads to hatred and, often, murder. Rosamel was a master of this kind of hypocrisy. His smile turned my stomach and I had to make an effort to keep quiet and harness my hands, which were always going for his throat.

I had just met my wife: she was a calm young thing, sweet, the color of cinnamon, dark-eyed, dressed in blue with white shoes; she carried one hand in a sling because she'd burned it. She smoked twisting her neck and wrinkling her brow. I was always trying to get her into a desperate dialog. But she didn't take me seriously. My inconsistency bothered her: in those days, in love, I waited for her hidden among the trees, doing everything possible so that, when she came up the hill, the whole bay would be behind her, the red bridge and the sun. Then she came as if she'd sprung from a test tube, sort of dreamlike, and I followed her around the concrete bumps until night filled up with a blue air, smelling of lilacs and the sounds of sirens driving away the fog; the sailboats froze, frost climbed the docks, the hills, the eucalyptus trees. And I took her by the hand. I knew her scar by heart. It ran from her thumb over the back of her hand like the veins of a dry leaf. At first I kissed it the way one kisses a parchment; but later the acid disappeared and only the inside of the leaf remained and I ran my tongue over it.

Rosamel observed me ironically: he understood that relationship from his widower's point of view. He'd lost a woman he had shacked up with for six months. For me that woman had no face, she hardly had the shape of a schoolteacher, a certain chubbiness and the warmth of old bedsheets. She died on Rosamel on account of medical ignorance. She had arrived hemorrhaging at the emergency room. They wrapped her in white bandages. She dyed everything red. The doctors persisted. She got redder. Finally, unable to stop the bleeding, they shut her into a wooden box, nailed down the sides, tightened it up and gave it to Rosamel. Suspicious, he could see through the hinges that his woman was still leaking, but much less now, until she finally dried up and they buried her. When I caressed my wife, it set Rosamel's teeth on edge.

One night two policemen dragged me back to my room and, unable to open the door, went into Rosamel's flat to get his help. I was out cold. The policemen tried to wake Rosamel and he started punching and kicking them. He defended himself like a madman, growling and groaning, wrapped in the sheets with the others trying to smother him. The policemen left me on the floor and beat him back. When I came to, I sat there watching Rosamel, who was dreaming about his grandmother, his mama and stepfather. This man was a clerk in a clothing store and kept his wife in line by means of hunger: he tied her to a table where he gave her liquids on a plate but nothing to eat. She'd taken on the color of aquavit, the same transparency, the same smell of burnt sugar and alcohol; her breasts had gone flat and her belly had grown a point like a rugby ball. Rosamel entered the dining room keeping himself hidden. He was a boy of nine, bald, extremely skinny, and he appeared to be wrapped in a thick beige sweater that came to his knees. His short pants didn't cover his scars. He wore black boots. Coming in he looked around and I noticed his detached philosophical air, his widower's sadness. The clothing store clerk lit into him and the blows sounded hollow. The man clamped his hands around Rosamel's pointy little head. His grandmother watched from the kitchen door, shaking her head and drying her hands in her black skirt. Rosamel wiped the snot from his face. His mother slipped, sweating, off her plate. "This photo," Rosamel told me, "was taken of my grandmother before they killed her. Look at that look. She looks like she's about to scream, doesn't she?" In fact, sticking her head out between his mother, the clothing store clerk and Rosamel, with the statue of General Baquedano and the Andes in the background, his grandmother could already see the murderer's claws. The dream was repeated several times and Rosamel groaned, whispered things and twitched under the sheets. His stepfather kept pummeling him all night. Little by little, the dream got shorter. Only his stepfather hit him and his grandmother wiped away the snot. Later it was just the stepfather and after that just the snot. With the morning light the stepfather turned to snot and the snot into a word Rosamel wouldn't say, and finally he woke up tired.

"How come the cops brought you?" he asked me.

"For the same reason as always. These two cops have been after me for twenty years. The one called Luis, with the long fangs, stiff hair, damp mustache, whose belly covered his chin, jumped out of broom closets sometimes and, without saying a word, piled up my secret things all around my feet until I couldn't move. Then he filed them away and sealed the file. The other cop, let's call him Arturo, then took the things out, went through them making astounded gestures and burned them. His white hair had been turned yellow by tobacco smoke, his legs got skinnier, his feet grew and he lost his memory."

Then I asked Rosamel, "What was the word you couldn't say last night?"

"It wasn't a word but a sentence my grandma said to me while watching me eat breakfast. She said: 'This kid's more a breadpooper than a milksipper.' "

Suddenly Rosamel married Veronica. I think he'd had enough of stepfathers.

"The other day this woman gave me a comb."

"Me too," I said to him, really surprised.

"She gave you a comb?"

"Yeah, she slid it under the door."

"And how do you know it was her? It could have been some other woman, or a man."

"I don't think there's more than one woman in this house who goes around giving out combs."

Rosamel got furiously jealous but contained himself. He invited me to the wedding but I didn't go. I should have gone. Rosamel had been best man at my wedding. Besides, before getting married he lived with us for a year. I remember we studied Socrates's suicide together, we figured out who killed him and prepared a *Dialogue* in which we exposed the facts and asked the Greek Consulate to reopen the case. My wife served us breakfast in bed and then brought out pipes and lit the fire for us. It was a honeymoon for all three of us. Rosamel watered the plants, cooked lentils, told stories about his grandmother and stepfather. I read aloud, washed his socks, we drank hot wine with oranges together and accompanied my wife to mass. We were a holy family. But I didn't go to his wedding.

Later things began to get hectic: one afternoon, about two years into the marriage, Rosamel called me and I went to see him. He lived in a pretty little white house. I mean in a cave inside another cave. He was worried, pacing, hands behind his back, talking about things that sounded incoherent to me. I thought I detected the intention of coming back to live with us. "And your wife?" That was the million dollar question. Then it seemed that it was I who was supposed to come live with him and his wife. "And leave my wife?" That was the other million dollar question. "No," he replied. I had the impression that Rosamel was talking about a band of individuals who lived communally and moved through the corridors of the house, up and down the stairs, over the roofs and in the basements, preaching. But we'd have to leave our wives. "No," he said, "they'll manage our band, we'll hand the money over to them, we'll cook for them, they'll fuck us, we'll take care of the kids for them and, when the time comes, they'll look after our ashes and polish the silverware. And as far as the kids are concerned, they'll be programmed from birth."

We were in the living room and Rosamel walked close to the door now, looking at it carefully, listening and stepping away again. He seemed to be sniffing something out. His little eyes were asking something for which there was still no answer. But a moaning could be heard behind the door and Rosamel ran and put his hand on the knob. I came closer too. Rosamel opened the door a crack and peeked. He turned to me and motioned with his mouth that I should look. Veronica was in bed with her sweater pulled up to her chin but otherwise totally naked, her legs were spread and between her legs she had a redheaded man she was milking the juice out of, clutching his freckled red butt with both her hands.

Rosamel closed the door again and went back to pacing. This scene began to repeat itself. I mean, every afternoon Rosamel paced the floor expounding on the goodness of the new sect, opening the door and showing me Veronica in bed with her legs wide open engulfing some guy of whatever color, guys tangled up in pants and socks and suspenders, she moaning like crazy, louder all the time, they plunging deep in her bones in search of the button that made her shake. Veronica became very familiar and friendly to me, I slowly began to identify her features and the tone of her cries. When Rosamel opened the door, I stuck my head in and gave her a friendly nod. But I never managed to see her standing up: only on her back and once or twice on top, going up and down, her hair over her face, smiling. Something else started repeating itself too: Rosamel went walking around the cellars at night. I remembered Cuzco. He went like a blind man, covered with flies, sniffing the vents that smelled of algae, of tar and moldy wood, feeling the wind waving in his face. Socrates came to be an obsession. Socrates prescribed him Librium and Thorazine, he gave him his private phone number saying he should call anytime, night or day, in case of despair.

Obviously he was afraid Rosamel would finally find the door and be gone.

Meanwhile honors kept falling on Rosamel and his bedroom; at the foot of the bed the money was piling up. His wife got fatter: her breasts, round and pink, bathed athletes in milk, her legs crushed them like boa constrictors, a steam rose from her crotch that dampened the ceiling until it dripped a milky liquid. Mushrooms started springing up out of the clothes and the walls. Veronica's eyes grew shiny, her mouth kept opening further and her tongue never stopped gleaming. At night Rosamel went over his earnings. All afternoon he talked nonstop about the butts of his visitors whom, naturally enough, he knew only from behind.

But this had to stop: Rosamel kept walking faster and faster up and down the halls. He opened the bedroom door now and again, stood there for a long time watching, then started pestering the couple. One guy got up out of bed and belted him. Rosamel cried that night, crumpled on the floor clutching his wife by the legs. She looked him over in her own way and when she spoke her voice was full of disdain. Rosamel wrote letters and left them unsigned. He bought a thick cable and got hold of a big empty box. He made a pact with me: not a gentleman's agreement this time, but a pact of the crucified. At the proper time I would set out on a journey, accompanied by a band of other madmen, preaching; we'd reach the foot of the mountain at the moment of his crucifixion; we'd see him taking the big leap and, if possible, save him. If that wasn't possible, we'd leap together.

One Thursday night Rosamel got out of bed while his wife was sound asleep. He crossed the living room and went down to the basement. He walked around a long time looking around in familiar corners. He communed with the open spaces in the air ducts, glimpsed the crowns of trees and cloudy skies, heard the night sirens, noises he knew from another time and country. He was getting used to the silence and the distance, like an athlete about to throw the discus, losing his way, gently cutting off all his clothes, bit by bit embracing the domain of lights arriving from far away, like a sailor who spreads his sails and lets them go while the rope slides swiftly burning through his hands. He sat down at a table and wrote a few disjointed words. He threw the papers in the waste basket. Then he wrote on the wall with chalk: *Greenwich Meridian, we never understood one another.* He left his watch on the table, got up, took the cable he'd hidden under some sacks, took the empty box, looked for a good beam, threw the cable over it, made a gigantic necktie knot, put his head through the loop, climbed on the box and jumped. His Adam's apple cracked and the lights went out.

I flew in with all the apostles in such a disorganized formation that we looked like flies. We came down on a yellow terrace facing the beach. We shook off the road dust, left our wings on a hanger and entered the mortuary parlor. Rosamel, seated, holding up his jaw with his hands, his head bent, watched us come in and sit down. An organist with gray gloves played a tango, "Uno." A Pentacostal pastor stood in the pulpit speaking, with particular reference to the sentences of the *Dialogue* that Rosamel and I had left unfinished. "It troubles me," he said, "that a man, a foreigner no less, should open the door that Socrates also opened and pass through into the beyond. As if one could enter the house of death through a window!"

Just then an enormous green curtain started flapping and, blowing in the direction of the gardens, fluttered with a sound like the sea.

"Is there anyone in this room opposed to the wedding of Rosamel with the holy church?" The question struck me as rhetorical and loaded. Nevertheless, I thought of my lovely Catholic years, of the Sunday trances, the thick smell of incense, the spilled wax on the white, blue and gold sashes as we filed into the ivory church.

I remembered the cold air brushing our faces and our new shoes slipping on the slabs of the freshly waxed floors. I was nine years old. I looked out the corner of my eye at the central nave filled with people and imagined myself a penitent monk. I really felt like martyr—so young, so sensitive!—and I lowered my eyes feeling that the devotees would melt faced with my incredible sufferings. We crossed the nave and occupied the benches at the foot of the altar. Then there was a hungry moment when my stomach growled in confusion, a sense of dizzy nausea mixed with the dense perfume of the lilies and the bitter smell of the vestry. The priest came in with his choirboys and started saying mass between his teeth. Red wrinkles formed on my knees. I often looked at my companions' backs and recognized the grass stains on their pants from playing hooky in the hills. The moment of consecration threw me, like now, up into the rarefied air of the dome and slammed me like an empty sack against the stained glass windows and celestial people—blue, white, bearded, winged—stuck like wafers to the walls and ceiling. I surrendered myself in the arms of the priest dressed in his white gown, starched and embroidered, like a baby at his baptism; I rested my face in his green or purple velvet, I smelled the chalice, the tray, I stuck out my tongue and received the fresh host like a crust of bread kneaded at dawn and swallowed with my eyes shut already thinking of the wafers I'd eat later in the park and the girl who'd go with me up to the dark benches under the trees, to suck each other's mouths.

I thought of saying: Yes, I'm opposed, on principle. But I was afraid. Rosamel's head was in a box and it looked out like the head of the spider woman at carnivals. I felt him scolding me. Not with anger, but something worse: an obstinate judgment, an implacable presence. In fact, I'd arrived late. I wasn't the redeemer nor the messiah he expected. But he'd forgotten about me and when he climbed into the box he wasn't thinking about me or his disciples. He was thinking about his wife. Now I was thinking about my wife too. Rosamel had fallen in love with her, with part of her: the part with which my wife loved me. Rosamel, from a distance, understood that he deserved that part, not me; or that I could settle for some other part, but the best, the biggest and juiciest, should belong to him. But he never said anything. He just looked. And the sharing of parts never came to be.

Now he'd gotten inside me and my wife in a curious way. He came in like a black cat and silently took his place. Or like a kind of crybaby, aggressive, drunken incoherence. I'd go down to the basement at night, any night, and open the doors and go out shouting into the street, stumbling and looking for a car to throw myself in front of. Or I'd get up out of bed, go into the bathroom and start piling up pills in my hand ready to swallow them. "If you don't open the door, they'll have to pump your stomach," said my wife. Several times I threw myself out the window—never the real window but the fake windows painted on the walls.

Rosamel had other intentions and I knew what they were: his plans included a rope and a box and my Adam's apple. Not finding his hang-up in me, he started looking for it in my wife. Lighter than me, frailer and more clairvoyant, devoted to her hormones, in continuous dispute with beings from the beyond by way of masses, prayers and confessions; she was possessed by Rosamel all the way. When I kissed her at night, she jumped like a frog, she blushed, her eyes clouded over and she curled up in a corner drawing pictures of heaven on the floor with her finger. She got up and walked around in circles for whole nights, days, weeks. Her face and her tongue dried up, she went pale, she took a razor and cut people, spattering blood on the books, the walls, the chairs. She took a running dive head-first against a closed window, she picked the pieces of broken glass off the floor and shook them at me in a rage, she slammed herself against the door and bit her knuckles. Finally, Rosamel got tired and went back to his other world, and my wife fell asleep twitching.

Enemas and fasting and x-rays did us no good at all. Rosamel wouldn't go away. Planted in me and my wife, he wove his threads, prepared his hangman's hood, called us to the funeral.

He figured out ways to surprise us. He'd erupt at midnight, or in the afternoon, or early in the morning. He'd come in smashing windows, moving tables around, pounding on doors. I went out one night on the way to throw myself off the bridge. We both got tired en route. I poured out some pills. They fell out of my hand. My wife was the first to realize Rosamel had gone.

One night I opened the door to the roof and threatened to jump. My wife spoke to me tenderly. We talked all night, she smoking and me with the door open looking down to the pavement below. Another night, my wife in her nightgown looked at me trembling and feverish all of a sudden and said: "I can't find the razor." Rosamel was gone. He'd gone, taking everything that was his: his rope, his box, his odor, his window, his razor and his face.

Veronica, who was neither dumb nor lazy, married the Monk. We forgot exactly what Rosamel was like and why we'd known him. He went away leaving just an old photo where he appeared in a sweater and flannel pants beside a lake, smiling nostalgically. I began to get fat. My wife had her tubes tied. Now, after all this time, I can hear a song, barely a tune. I pick up the guitar thinking of Rosamel and together we sing about those days, we smile thinking that even a hanged man can sometimes become a tree, a beloved shade, so far away, and then forgotten, or not forgotten, like that green curtain billowing in the wind and flapping furiously against the sea.

The Fall of a Bishop

All right, then. Like Saint Augustine, beloved brothers, I was a guitar player, a soldier, an executioner, a photographer, a convert, Veronica's husband, lover of Pia and the Monk. I followed the path of the flesh like a dog of the Lord: *Domini canis*.

First, I left the Mission to serve as an inventor of metaphysics in a neighborhood seminary. Soon it came to be said of me that I'd turned proud, overbearing, eager to be a bishop. When asked I answered firmly, without hesitation: "Yes, Father, I renounce life, bring on the cassock." I was a meek and simple novice but an insolent sexton. Gray-haired at thirty, thin, with clear eyes, a swordsman's hands and skinny legs that Pia adored, I knew how to wear my black robe and silk shirtfront elegantly. During the first year of metaphysics I committed certain indecent acts: I slapped the Father Superior around; I wrote an article, which was reprinted in the red and yellow press, about the Order's swindlings of the Treasury and the novices' wild parties. But my worst trespass was to be surprised spying on the young ladies of Bethany College, who bathed in the nude at five in the morning and went back to their exercises dripping wet. I was considered a little perverted and was punished. I spent two years doing domestic chores, dragging myself from the courtyards to the classrooms, from the classrooms to the kitchen, from the kitchen to the infirmary. I swept, I cooked, I washed, I scrubbed, until, after a few years, I rebelled. I asked to be excused, going through normal channels. I sent my official requests to Rome by hand and the replies came back to me on foot. "Poveretto Oblato, you have nothing to ask for nor hope for, there is the window: you entered like a vagabond at nightfall, leave like a pariah, the night is beginning." Furious, made fun of, offended, I resolved to confront my enemies in person. I should add that, in that last year, I fell madly in love with an Italian widow, whose confidante I was and in whose green eyes I got lost for entire afternoons, opening and closing doors, saving and burning papers, collecting rings and expense accounts, counting the days in the rhythm we danced, half naked, in her car.

Finally I cut out. One day, fed up with hypocrisies and intrigues, I took my hat, my coat and my suitcase and went out on Potrero Avenue. I was received in grand style. I was the deacon of a little adobe church, with red rooftiles and oak balconies. My priest had a mahogany desk, cedar shelves, cabinets full of port and sherry, leatherbound books, felt easy chairs, velvet couches. All of which was like my own. The parishioners surrounded me with affection: the chorus of girls sang for me at dawn; the gentlemen from Columbus collected money and we played poker; the widow brought her children on Friday nights and cooked me polenta, golden and fragrant.

This couldn't go on. My face was falling off with shame. I heard confessions, I gave out blessings like a ship's cook hidden under seven decks of passengers. My sermon smelled like wine and onions. I never spoke of God, whom I didn't know, but of the needs of the building, the benches of the school, the orchestra on Saturdays, the temperature of the refrigerator. I hid my learning. I spruced myself up especially for midnight mass. I began to receive proposals of marriage, invitations to dine, bottles of cologne. I told the Italian not now, she had many children and it wouldn't be right for a priest. I fell in love with a young nurse, with her pale vain face, her veiled smile. We discussed philosophy, she sitting on my lap, listening to Bach, smoking

Turkish cigarettes and drinking sherry. I discovered that in her company I couldn't control my hands or my legs. I took her by the neck and made her dance. "You don't dance to Bach," she told me. But I had seen couples dancing holding one another by the ass, sucking each other's lips, their legs wrapped around each other. I took off the Bach and put on Gregorian chants. I rocked her and pushed her and, since I couldn't keep the rhythm, I slammed her against the walls and banged her on the head. She laughed at me, putting out and lighting cigarettes, throwing the sherry on the floor, flicking ashes on my shirtfront. My face trembled, my mouth twisted, I tried to drag her into the bedroom and she, frightened, said, "What's the matter with you, you're having an attack, here, sniff this hanky." I yelled and went spinning around the room, dancing the way I thought they danced in the world, keeping an eye on her. I burned my fingers, my feet got tangled up and I fell, finally, like a dog in search of a lap. But I was shaking too hard and I ripped her stockings. She picked up her things and left on the run.

    I decided to get married. I renounced the parish. I took a job as a chaplain in order to be closer to her. In the months it took these changes to occur, she wrote me conciliatory messages. In one she said I should try to fornicate morning, noon and night, with a great variety of persons, because my nervousness and my doubts were due to lack of experience, and my haste due to an excessive amount of semen, and my dances due to the pressure of this semen inside me with no way out. I carefully considered the advice. I proceeded to find out where one could fornicate with such authority. They told me Tijuana. I left for the sinful city.

    I got there in the morning, and playing the devil, I went into a tavern for a drink. The women came over, offering themselves. In order to gain experience, I decided to marry the smallest, most timid and withdrawn one, whose name was Lucia and whose black hair fell loosely down her back to her little white knees. Lucia threw her legs over mine, she touched my lips with her nipples, she took my hand and placed it on her moist brown crotch. My marriage proposal made her laugh, but she didn't tell anyone, she kept it between her gold teeth and waited. I went out to find a taxi and told the driver my secret. The man looked me over carefully and shook my hand. Thanking me, he called me Father. I, who'd disguised myself as a cowboy, decided he must have seen me once in the parish and recognized me. Lucia and I left in the taxi to take out our marriage license. The ceremony was brief. I paid for the stamp and the judge pronounced us man and wife.

I was married to Lucia for a year. We lived in a fourth floor flat, with three beds, a woodstove, six children (all hers) and her mother, a bald-headed Indian who made tortillas on a stone and sold lottery tickets. Lucia danced all night. During the day I tried not to let her sleep, but she convinced me with her fists that we'd only fuck during business hours, paid in advance with the pesos I started earning as a busboy in the kitchen of the cabaret.

I won't say I was unhappy in this house, not any more or less than the rats and cockroaches in the corners. I didn't mind the smell of the children, I didn't itch, I didn't eat too much, and the cold didn't bother me like it did the Indian. I put newspapers under my shirt, I patched the holes in my shoes with cardboard, I bought myself a hat and cowboy spurs.

From time to time, I wrote to my far-off sweetheart, reporting on my progress. She'd forgotten me. I began to feel that, little by little, I was becoming a Tijuana husband. But Lucia had other plans for me. She left her job as a dancer and started working from noon to four, like a doctor; she took twenty pesos a throw, which included a purple acidy wine called Alvino; she received her customers in a nightshirt; she raised her legs very high; she used rubber devices, plastic coils, paper towels. Her patients were soldiers, students, policemen and a foreigner lady or two. The bald-headed Indian changed the towels, dried the floor, shook out the sheets. I brought the clients in a taxicab, brushed off their dandruff, cleaned the bathroom, collected the money and if I had to sing, I sang. I would have taken this treatment forever but Lucia refused to fuck me. "Never again," she said. "If you want baldy, there she is. With me, never." I begged her, I got down on my knees weeping, I reminded her what she'd cost me, my career and my parishioners. She wasn't listening. She smoked the hash pipe she kept in her bosom, she scratched her head, combed her hair, sipped her tortilla soup, ate her fried beans and read the horoscopes. "Scratch me here," she said to me. And I, sitting on the floor, looking at her sagging breasts as dark and soft as figs, reached out my hand and scratched her, feeling I was still a bellringer and that I was ringing Vespers with my sore fingers and broken nails.

Lucia suffered bites that left ugly welts on the folds of her arms and legs. Little as she was, with big black eyes and spry as a tiger cub, she dreamed once of being an actress and fought fiercely to convince the world of her art. The directors assigned her to play an Indian orphan; she tried to be the lady of the camellias; she wanted to turn into a new Lola del Rio and work in silent movies on the basis of her moves and her looks. But her failure wasn't, finally, on the screen; it was on her honeymoon. Lucia had the tenderness of a little woman for big men, and for marriage she chose a reinforced concrete cowboy who never saw past the top of her head and as a consequence never appreciated the wealth of her affection or her delicate little heart. When the cowboy started spending all his days drunk as a lush and throwing his wife around, she slipped out of his hands; he couldn't work or think or fuck anymore, Lucia was covered with bruises and her tender gaze filled up with fear, her voice grew bitter and she started to talk in screams. She started buying and selling things and was jealous and dominating. She buried the cowboy with his boots on and became a dancer again.

One afternoon Gabriel appeared. He'd come to see Lucia and he was in a hurry but, after leaving his sword on the table, he heard me out. "I don't see what you're complaining about," said the shaggy old guy, "they feed you regularly, you have a bed to sleep in, children who respect you, a good mother-in-law and a little wife who keeps you warm." I explained my situation to him. Gabriel had taken his boots off and put his belt over the chair. "Listen, son, what you need is a missionary position. You're no good as a husband. You expected too much. You'll never learn to live with a woman now. Look at you. Anybody can see you've got the mark of a priest from a mile away. Your pants are baggy, your jacket doesn't fit, you've got a white collar and a penguin's shirtfront, kids are scared of you, dogs bark at you, you're not a man to the men and you're no woman to the women. Lucia's all out of milk, she's dried up. You should go back to your mission. You've fucked enough. Live on your memories now."

Gabriel took off his wings with an effort. "Carry the secret with you to the grave because you seem to have conquered peace: lovers breathe through their mouths. God knows more from being in love than the Devil does from being evil. There'd be no tombs without people like you. Nor secrets. Take it away, boy, this horny life isn't for you. Leave her to the tourists, the travelers who are always on the road. If you come back, come back unashamed, you've paid your dues. Go home."

Monk to your wafers, I said to myself then, and I came back to Potrero Avenue, and from there, wifeless, to the Mission, and everything started over again at last. I am a guy who talks and plays tricks.

The Bullfight

But along comes a magistrate talking about the war, a magistrate with a white hat, an admiral's frock coat, a sword, bluejeans and boots. He arrives by helicopter and it tries to land on the terrace. A huge crowd has gathered, made up mostly of police cars, spies and national guardsmen with fixed bayonets. And my students. It's hard to describe their outfits, but here goes.

The girls: long tunics in many colors, loose hair, wooden earrings, leather or goatskin boots, and under the dresses, hanging from their waists, soap bubbles and marijuana bushes.

The boys: they also wear long unwashed hair, go barefoot, with vests like Buffalo Bill, big Dracula capes, Superman pants, hunter's hats, beards and tambourines. The tabs of acid come in two sizes: big and bad.

The helicopter prepares to land. The flags with stars and stripes flutter atop the greased poles. A band plays the battle charge. The helicopter looks for its circle of chalk. The machine's blades roar, raising a tremendous gust of wind and lots of dust. Now it's about to land. Then the students come running and fill up the chalk circle. The helicopter looks down, hesitates, hangs there awhile and goes back up. It makes an elegant turn around the terrace and repeats the procedure. The students don't move. The helicopter tries to shave them with its blades. It goes up again. This happens several times. Until the public gets bored. Then the helicopter heads toward the opposite end of the terrace.

The students run over there and fill up the other chalk circle. The helicopter, furious, heads further out. But the students get there before it does. The helicopter roars, screeches, flies from one side of the terrace to the other, looking like an ordinary dragonfly, and tries to force its way into the circle. But the circle is full of students. Now, helicopter and students are running all over the city, the helicopter looking for a clearing and the students denser and denser like a forest. The public laughs loudly and applauds the bullfight.

A note on the landscape: the official platform stands beside the city fountain. The guerrillas have filled the lions with urine and these pee throughout the ceremony.

The Constitutionalists

Meanwhile a fence was growing around my place and it wasn't the work of masons or carpenters but of persons employed by the government as pioneers, protestants and soldiers. It was also growing out of my body, I have to admit, since I was walking around like those medieval towers, covered with turrets and pontoons, armed with gauntlets, looking for a place to collapse crushing the enemy.

The letters from my wife were never delivered because, when they asked me who I was and where I came from, they tried to see themselves in my face and what they saw made them mad. He's a son of a bitch, they said, and the echo in my face said back: He's a son of a bitch. So we were both sons of bitches. But I went around all over the place with my face, and the echo of course went from face to face, along hallways, through offices, lobbies, churches, schools, barracks, hospitals, so that by the end of the day we were thousands of sons of bitches and, by Christmas, millions, and without being able to become accustomed to our condition and accept the name as properly familiar, the insults and spitting followed, and sometimes violence.

What do you have against these people? That was the first question in my interior dialogue, and the answers often took the form of syllogisms, for example:

"A was born among hogs in Italy; B grew up packing hog

meat in Chicago; C settled in New York, bought a house, a car and new teeth. C married A. Ergo, C is a hog." To which I would add: "A and B, through blood relations with C, are also hogs."

Another syllogism:

"Polack A likes sausage and beer and has an M-1 rifle he uses for shooting blacks; German B suffers from piles and hates A (whom he once went after with a wrench); C is the founder of America First and goes hunting with A. Ergo, B's piles are operable in the case of A, but not in the case of C." To which I would add: "All three can go take a shit, i.e., A, B and C."

One more syllogism, this one of the compound kind:

"A, B and C, triplets de jure but not de facto, have discovered a country that can be completely paved, over which a smokescreen can be hung and whose holes can be patched with the pelts of animals hunted in winter; they divide it into houses (funeral homes, nuthouses, orphans' homes, old people's homes, houses of ill repute, houses of representatives, houses for rent, homes with two baths, homes for the disabled, all-electric homes, convalescent homes, white houses); these houses are sold to D, E and F with 100 year mortgages, at 12% interest for every time they enter the house and 6% (compounded) every time they go out; D, E and F burn down these houses; G, H and I, being neither lazy nor foolish, start a fire department; J, K and L start an insurance company; M, N and O, the shrewdest of all, become police officers and start collecting wages from A, B, C, D, E, F, G, H, I, J, K and L, but L steps forth and declares the houses unhealthy, opens a jail and arrests D, E and F for arson. M, not to be outdone, declares a state of emergency and, supported by N and O, also known as O the Oink, take over, invent a Pentagon, declare war on P, Q and R and go off to kill Asians, but when R comes back he tells M, Go fuck yourself, to which S, who was just waiting for the chance, declares the country's independence and electrocutes T, gives a speech in the United Nations and sends off a battalion of Marines to boil Indians in LSD. U, V and X declare themselves pacifists; Y organizes the YMCA. Ergo, Z is the last letter in the alphabet. In other words, the world's asshole."

This couldn't go on. The whole country was fucking me over. I distrusted everyone and they all distrusted me. Women took on a curious role: they approached me with their legs pressed shut. Well-groomed, sweet-smelling, healthy and elegant, dressed like stewardesses or nurses or housewives, they'd see me and flash their teeth and shut their legs. They were trying to trick me into raping them. But instead I just grinned, tickled them a little, worshipped them and, as soon as their guard was down, pried their legs open.

The country's constitution explains this very clearly. It says:

"In this country the citizens (male) shall turn out the light to do their business, they shall carry an account book where they shall log their erections and a stamp book to keep track of the fucks their wives grant them. This power shall give the wife the right of original sin. The bed shall be a stretcher for the sick husband; the wife shall close her eyes and hold her nose; she shall be allowed neither to tease nor to come; she shall wash immediately and wipe herself dry with tissue. Husband and wife shall have a quarter of a child every five years. They shall be assisted by coils, hooks, rubbers and pills. The citizen shall be able to masturbate or purchase pussy on the street. Once the four quarters of the child are assembled, its mother shall care for it in bottles. The citizen shall die without having seen his wife's thing. He shall not know whether the door of life is vertical or horizontal, nor why she, his wife, moaned one time when he fucked her on the floor. The citizen shall develop allergies to his wife, such as rashes, itching, sneezing, sores and asthma. His wife shall give the citizen a heart attack.

"In case of divorce, the citizen shall hand over to his wife: his automobile, his house, his salary, his bed, his wig and his vitamins. The wife shall return to the husband her toothbrush and a pair of stockings. The citizen shall pay his premiums and the wife shall have her life insured. In cases of extreme cruelty, death shall be prorated in equal parts. In cases of incompatibility, adultery, impotence, abandonment and incest, the citizen shall pay for his own funeral. The wife shall be able to order him cremated but not to keep the ashes. These shall be used as fertilizer in Astrodomes.

"If the citizen should abuse his physical weakness exceeding the allotted number of caresses either with hand, fingers, knees or feet, the wife shall have the right to administer two lashes for each offense, taking care not to strike his private parts.

"Woman is sacred. Whoever says otherwise has to prove it."

The Constitution sets all this down with plenty of political and economic reasons but without shedding much light on my problem. I understand that such phenomena as I've described occur, but at the same time I can't help but see that they're softening me up, they're making my hair fall out, they're hurting me in some essential way that's going to make me a cripple. I don't talk much, and when I do it's in one-syllable words. I groan a lot. I beat my family, sometimes barehanded, sometimes with a strap.

"How often?" asks the father confessor.

"Every day."

"How?"

"I already said, with my hand or with a strap."

"With a stick?"

"No."

"Why?"

"What do you mean, why?"

"What for."

"Nobody knows why they beat their family, do you?"

"I don't beat mine. Do you repent?"

"With all my heart. With all my heart."

"You won't do it again?"

"Never again."

"Pray a hundred Our Fathers."

Then I went back to doing it, beating them harder every time.

I'm telling you this couldn't go on.

My wife was getting skinny, her legs were shaky, the light was leaving her eyes, she fell asleep at the stove. Then she started to hit back. Her fist connected, stunned me. The kids wouldn't let me near them. They started to see me as an old stranger, a kind of wandering Jew their mother put up with. They didn't trust me. They listened to me like some carnival barker: the bear keeper, the man with the monkey who tells fortunes. They wound up convincing me I was an organ grinder. I began to suffer alone, crying, thinking about my old friend Cuzco, giving speeches on patriotic occasions, babbling about my wedding night. Finally they left me to myself. Then I got drafted.

The Autopsy

The corridors are full of men in undershorts. We move forward slowly, our bare feet slipping over the floor like toads. At the end of the corridor a red eye flashes on and off, a bell rings, the doors open. There is a sound of scissors and injections. Arriving at the red eye, we lose our shorts. In front of us, thousands of men waiting, and thousands behind and thousands on the walkways and thousands in the cellars and thousands on the roofs. A smell of pale sherry and freshly cut hay and leather and combs begins to circulate, stirred by wooden propellers. We're sweating. The walls absorb the sweat and it drops to the floor in puddles taking on a creamy color. A trapdoor opens in the floor and we fall through. Cuzco, Rosamel and me in a laboratory. A woman in white with steel-rimmed glasses focuses on us through an enormous Kodak which she operates with levers and lead switches. She inserts and removes plates, ties us up with rubber straps, hides under a black rag and takes our picture hung up by the neck. Then she looks up our ass. She laughs. She gives us porcelain jars and wooden spoons, puts a label on our wrist and attaches a little violet bell to our tool.

Another woman, this one younger, pale and ethereal, looks us over for a second with her tortoise-shell eyes and then begins to measure our ears and, like a queen bee in her hive, extracts wax which she places in matchboxes. She invites us to be seated. I'm not sure whether I should cross my legs, like Rosamel, because my balls get squished. Cuzco's keeping quiet, covering himself with his hands.

"Pay close attention," says the queen bee, and sticks an earphone in our ear, "pay close attention." She hits our knees with a little silver hammer, our chin, our elbows and the soles of our feet. "Listen carefully. What do you hear?"

"I hear bells ringing, fading away, washing out; now it's a scraping sound, a flea jumping in my ear, a flea that never comes down."

"Fine."

"I hear bells ringing, a meteorite falling, a leaf falling from a tree, a man falling over backwards, a wave in a silent film."

"Fine."

"I hear bells ringing, a burnt-out electric chair, a cotton boll opening, the roof coming off, the door opening but nobody comes in, somebody's peeking through the keyhole."

The nurse sticks her fingers in my ears, she pokes around and observes my reactions. She makes a notation in her book. "Now," she says, "write down the words you hear on this piece of paper." The words come in through the earphones. I can't understand them. They're a big jumble. We don't write anything down. The queen bee looks at the paper, takes accounts and writes: *Deaf.*

Now we move to the inside of a closet. Seated on a little bench ther's a man in a white apron, with a sad look and gray hair. He invites us to lie down on a cot. We lie down. He takes out some tubes and puts them to his ears and, since he's tapping his foot, I figure he's listening to music. He lets us talk. It's crucially important that this man testify to our ills and place his signature and his stamp on our death certificates, because we won't be going to war: even if we have to be epileptics, sodomites or lepers.

"My stomach's in backwards," I say, "and the winds won't leave me alone, they come and go through me like hurricanes, top to bottom, side to side, filling me up, emptying me, turning my guts over, puncturing arteries, smashing kidneys."

"I've got a bad heart."

"Ah! And you, how come you're wiggling so much?"

"I have St. Vitus dance, I've got chills, I dropped a leg and when I go back to get it the other one falls off, I kick things, I break whatever I touch, I shake, I bump into walls, I scare cats, I'm possessed."

"Well, you're very much alive."

"Uh, I don't know, but . . . please excuse my erection; I'm not used to lying down naked with strangers and being felt all over like this. Besides the young lady stuck her finger in me from behind, and finally I have this letter from my private physician."

The man puts on his glasses, looks at the letter. "Are you a sodomite?"

"The letter, sir, read the letter."

"I read it. I repeat, are you a sodomite?"

"I take the Fifth Amendment. Read the letter."

"I read it. Bend over."

"I won't."

"Bend over."

"I'll scream. You want me to?"

"You won't dare."

"Hold me down."

"Hold whom down?"

The three of us hold down the man in white, we shove him on to the cot, we bend over him. The man in white keeps time with his foot.

Home for the Holidays

I'm twenty-four years old with a wide forehead and long curly hair; I'm also my thin, wiry, beady-eyed wife, and am myself heavy, slow and chubby. Inside the brick building, which is riddled with holes and more or less demolished, it's a dark midnight but bathed in the light of the searchlights and the flames, the three of us are waiting for the attack of the little elephants that will come charging in, knocking down the barricades, breaking down the doors with their big gray feet, farting and blowing their horns. We're sitting on the floor and they walk right over us, they surround us and drag us by the hair and we go bounding down the concrete stairs. My wife and I try to get close to each other but we're separated by huge bonfires where chairs, windowframes and desks are burning. The flames roar and we step back. The bells are ringing in the campanile. The black panthers beat their drums with their fists and elbows, a chorus of flutes rises from the eucalyptus trees, stars shoot over at a low altitude, the heroic girls offer their breasts singing. Yellow buses go rumbling by; I look through the bars but can't make out any faces. My father walks away marking each step with his cane, my mother takes his arm, both of them dressed in black, and they start to float off like balloons, my mother turning somersaults in the air, her tiny feet attached to a round body. Our gloves exploding in the rain, we take off at high speed. I'm calm. Calmly I remove my clothes, lie down and drop immediately into a dreamless sleep. I wake up at five in the morning. Twenty-six years have gone by, my wife's still awake, her hair's gone gray and she's wrinkled. We live uneasily in this wax museum.

The elephants put the fires out with their feet. They turn into pigs. The crowd pelts them with beer cans. The buses take off in the night, their sirens wailing. Dawn at Santa Rita. So much for towers and bridges, the fields of barley and clover begin, the celery farms on the outskirts of Milpitas. A cow is smoking next to the bars; the prisoners, dressed in blue, are washing the floor. They take away our clothes and make us lie down in the yard. My house looks sort of like Santa Rita now. I'm living in Santa Rita tied to an iron post. Somebody comes up and smashes my face against the post. I smile in the dark. I play chess with a murderer. The years go by and I learn not to beat him, but they throw him in the hole and after a while they poke him with a stick. He squirms around. And they throw him back in my cell.

I haven't changed that much: maybe lost a little hair, my teeth have sharpened a little, my neck has thickened and, sitting down, I could pass for a trash can. My parents throw me breadcrumbs over the fence and I pick them up with my mouth. Somebody slams a little kid against the fence. We can't even hear ourselves scream anymore. Boy, I say, everything's going to be fine. But I say it from a great height, gliding like an eagle over the yard at Santa Rita. My son sees me falling and smiles sadly. It's getting away from me, the yard gets smaller and smaller, it's nothing but a little rectangle down below and my son's standing there with his hands upraised and from here I can see the mountains, the sea and some bell towers, I hear my wife crying and now we're all up on the fence, clawing and gnawing our way over, trying to climb, but there's a lot of us and the fence is endless. My parents, walking very slowly, wave to me. They're close to the gate and my father starts knocking on it with his cane. He pays a hundred dollars a year. That's all he can afford. He sells his cigarettes, his wallet. They hand me a piece of paper and I sign. The walls of the jail lift up.

The sun's coming up and it's cold. The fog picks us up feet first. A car goes by with its lights on. The hills are already taking on clear outlines and the dew is beginning to gleam. Over the damp and frosty ground, from the depths of the country, on the far side of the fence, a boy comes walking, in a blue shirt and pants; they've taken away his shoes, the morning mist steams from his mouth, he sees me from a long way off and smiles, a flock of birds obscures him for a minute but he reappears and I rub my hands and stamp my feet to get warm. When we turn around we've both disappeared. The sun is shining. Years have gone by today. The kid has been in a fight. My quiet wife lights her cigarette. My parents think I've come home for good and won't go away again.

The Airmail Package

Since I came to this house there've been two things I thought would happen for sure: first, I knew I had *not* arrived at my final destination; second, I knew that the reason for my indeterminate sentence and my chances of getting out were hidden in the house itself, with other people I could count on to vindicate me if they'd just take off their masks. They could set me free if in an act of love we managed to bar the door, close off the halls and make this open sack of women, children, young couples, old folks and criminals look like a solid, secure house.

 I got fired from my posts of executioner, teacher and portrait painter on account of laziness. How couldn't I miss my little desk covered with papers and pencils and rubber bands, my wheelchair, my reading lamp, my typewriter full of hair, my calendar riddled with bulletholes, my window opening on a wall! "You didn't fill your quota of heads," the Bosswoman said to me. "Another wasted week. We've given you time and more personnel, better weapons, a new interpreter, a flaming village full of old people and children, a map of the caves and underground sewers in your new territory. But you failed again. What do you think you're doing? You think you can go on living inside your wife like a parasite? Do your work, earn your keep. Deliver your quota of heads. But it's no use. You're good for nothing." Then they assigned me to a reconnaissance patrol.

My Bosswoman had gotten fatter over the years: she was one big ball of tar, wrinkled and black, with piles of gray hair and thick glasses and incredibly high-heeled shoes. She had placed her desk on a platform hanging from the ceiling by four chains, and from up there, balancing, she commanded the whole office. At eight in the morning she blew reveille on a yellow bugle. Flags and feathers sprang out of nowhere. A drum rolled. They called our numbers. "How many heads have you got? You're a lazy bum," she said to me.

And her eye followed me everywhere: it was in my bed, it was stuck in the wall when I went to the toilet, it was in the seat of my pants, I could feel it in my chest and in my forehead. Sometimes I felt it from far away, up there in her cage, in the clouds, swaying in the summer breeze. I started to smile and stretch my legs. Just then reveille would play, the flags would unfurl, the drums rolled. "You're a good-for-nothing!" she yelled.

In order to earn my keep I started bringing her lots of heads. I came into the office dancing and with an extravagant gesture dumped the heads at her feet. I was the reaper who goes out over the quiet smoky fields in the evening shadows, leaving the sun going down alone among the cows, and strolling slowly heads down the road and comes back with a sack on his shoulder and doesn't stop until he gets to the houses and looks around and passes among the farmhands and the women, comes up to the little queen and takes off his black hat, and while the others deposit the celery, the beets, the grapefruits and eggplants at her feet, I emptied my basket full of heads and watched the giddy look on her face, feeling my tongue rub the roof of my mouth and my fingers clench in frustration.

Besides which, I'd taken on a tremendous family. I lost count. We lived in a room with beds on the floor, along the walls and in the closets. All of a sudden a skinny little thing would run between my legs, black, with kinky hair, running and yelling, with another one chasing him. I looked them over closely but didn't recognize them. "Who are they?" I asked. "Where do they come from? Where are they going? There's not enough food for them—or clothes or schools or jobs."

"You'll have to work harder."

But there was nothing else to do at the office. I bought a shovel and applied for a job at the cemetery. I went back to the plains, to the wide-open spaces, to the cypresses and eucalyptus I always loved, to the clover and the mustard, to the damp, soft, dense earth, the smell of rotting leaves crawling with worms. I worked from sunup to sundown: a well-established sun that got itself up with dignity like a veteran actor, coming out from behind the willows, waiting its turn in the San Pablo valley, reflected in reverse in dark lagoons and rising later to the peaks of the hills announcing itself with a flashy display of its rays, countershadows, sheets of glare, a sun that started in its own seat and wandered around looking for a spot in the shade, a sun that sank like a circus coffin into its huge hole in the sea. We were left with the posters, the robes, the shawls and the furs of a lot of people who left with the first gust of wind and trembled looking for a safe place under the shovels. I buried soldiers and my assistants nailed up flags. At nightfall, exhausted, our hands covered with calluses, our throats dry, our foreheads sweaty, we'd open a beer, go over to the oven, look through the window and watch the heroes burning. A hero went in laid out on his stretcher. They'd spread him out on the grill and the flame shot over him. He'd give a little jump. Or his arms would fly up. Then he'd go up in gorgeous flames; he'd fry to a crisp like a sparkler, his hair in the air, tongue on fire, belly crackling, legs burning a bit slower but flaring up just the same. We watched and we walked away. The human smoke curled from the chimney, wrapped itself around the eucalyptus and then floated off in search of the neighborhood skylights, flying into houses leaving ashes on the curtains, little personal smells, traces of a well-lived life, short but violent, a presence that didn't impose itself but simply breathed.

The kids grew up, my wife kept trying to give birth like an industry but by now she was skinny and toothless, just washing and mending with stiff fingers and toughened arms. I was getting blacker all the time, with an earthy obscurity and mole-like movements. I plucked my eyebrows, my beard was a tangle of roots. My oldest son came home drunk one night and I went out to block his way. He came back with a tremendous rock and heaved it at my chest. He threw it at me crying. Furious. I tried to subdue him but he was bigger and stronger than me. With several slugs he knocked me against the wall. Then he went out of the house, sat down on a stone a few feet from the window and spent the whole night howling. He was my favorite kid. My other kids, meanwhile, came home dying, or ran away, or became nurses or thieves, or got married. None of them wanted to work like their father—as a gravedigger—or like their mother—as a birthgiver. They didn't even speak our language anymore and they'd changed their way of hearing, of seeing, of walking. They'd slowed down, gotten more sure of themselves, they understood animals better. To them my wife and I were a couple of old clowns, tired old circus horses, soulless imposters.

All right. One December night, about four, four-thirty, the burglary hour, somebody knocked at the door. I got up, stumbling across the piled-up bodies all over the floor as always, and let him in: it was a soldier. A tall fellow, with a hat with lots of stars and a coat with lots of medals, not much of a face. He looked for a place to sit down. We pushed the wounded aside and found him a chair. "Today," he said, "our country was attacked by the yellow peril and your son was killed in a firefight. Here," he said to my wife, handing her a flag nicely folded like a sheet. "Here," he said to me, handing me my son's corpse wrapped in cellophane with lots of stamps and sealing wax. He had me sign a receipt and then he left.

Then, for a moment, there was nothing to do. There was one of those pauses like between the drops when you're trying to find the leak, or trying to figure out which one of the kids it is who's coughing. With the flag and the package on our laps we began to unwrap our son. Because that's what was expected of us. Our son—who was brown, curlyhaired, with sad hard eyes, with a nervous mouth, a tired gentle way with his body, waiting for a life that never came nor tried to reveal itself but went on slowly and secretly taking shape, like the space in the field where we pitch our tent without even knowing if there'll be other tents nearby or if we'll be left alone in the clearing; his mother now a glass on the table, his father a rug on the floor to warm his feet; our son keeping something to himself that ought to be spoken or touched, since faces and bodies had been maturing in him for awhile, which in turn would burst out crying or loving or living with us; our son laid out on his back in summertime looking up with a smile at the vines growing around his window, at the girls beginning to climb through the bars with their cool bare legs, and the children pushing their way out between those legs, stubborn and serious like little cyclists, our son—he had come to an end.

But the world is beginning to take on a slower rhythm, very steady, and the windows are multiplying, trees and books are taking root, chairs are reproducing. My wife has taken her child by the hand, she strokes his cheeks tenderly, she leans over him and spends years watching him, seeing the fever secretly come and go, the first steps toward the spring thaw, the shy flight over the straps of summer, his sea-changes tied to the dark nets of kelp the pelicans hold up calling, and she carries him with magical care among other children and other women and gives him her breast and combs his hair and hands him to me and the child laughs and runs and chases the earth kicking, and together we drink and celebrate. A miracle will happen in our child's life and everything's falling into place for just that purpose. Then the sun comes up, a kind of light comes out and shines down on our family. The miracle turns out to be a small one: my wife is always crying, now with a sheet full of stars in her hands. I'm next to her and the floor is covered with kids. On my lap I'm holding my favorite one, wrapped like an airmail package, with a tag that says: FRAGILE. THIS SIDE UP.

Changing Times

People started taking off their clothes, letting their hair grow, talking to God, denying the sanctity of money, the power of armies, the purity of stadiums, the innocence of the police. They began going out in parks in hordes: men, women, children, barefoot, filthy and lousy, praying and singing, banging on drums and whacking tambourines. The government called a meeting of bishops. It was a quick consultation. No need to get upset was their opinion. But executives, generals and deputy sheriffs wanted action. The people answered with their hair. Strange things happened: people jumped off bridges but didn't fall. Hotels emptied. Multitudes of whales washed up on the beaches. One day a barefoot man in a tank top, with shaggy hair and a beard, went into a bank. The government took measures: the police filled their mouths with tear gas, their guns with bullets, their holsters with guns and went out to fight barefoot men in tank tops who went into banks. Crowds sat down in front of the police. Millions of persons (not counting the old folks in their hammocks who could smell the war) sang hymns and smoked their stuff. Girls with glass masks danced on the marquees. Bands played, singers plugged in their guitars, the nation's women showed off their breasts, men took their clothes off in unexpected places and their pictures were taken embracing. It was the end of the private home. St. George crusaders, messengers, magicians, pirates, barbers, bullfighters and embalmers came in and out the windows. Over the world's fields grew acres of Acapulco gold and in the evenings, while the fields burned, clouds of marijuana smoke hovered around the mouths of horses and cows, engulfed rabbits and crows, and murmurs of love spread out in a hush. Airliners lost their way and landed in Cuba. It was the end of alcohol. At first the women put on colorful pants, later they took off the pants and wore a hanky around their waist. The men didn't know what to do: we let our beards grow, we undressed in theaters, but we didn't dare go out in miniskirts. The country was swaying from side to side, happy, high, dancing the golden age into existence. No more husbands and wives. Children were conceived in transit. Universities carried on lying down.

Finally the world was divided: on one side, people fucked on Saturday nights, went to church Sunday, deposited their money Monday, counted it Tuesday, interest went up Wednesday, they bought guns Thursday, collected the bodies Friday, and fucked on Saturday night; on the other side, people traded mates, bought little bells, saluted the rising sun, sat down in front of trains, did some time in jail, slept wherever they pleased, and forgot what color they were.

Crazy-eyed killers jumped out of towers, trees, moving cars, slaying people with chains, skinning their victims with knives, brandishing jawbones.

The government order:

"Persons who shave and keep their jobs and their wives and live in the suburbs surrounded by flowering trees and protected by police dogs may enter banks. They shall be recognized by their love for the flag, their smell and their illnesses. They shall eat any animals they please, raw or cooked. They shall preserve themselves in jars and enjoy their pensions as they see fit. On the other hand: *'Bullets for the beards.'* "

The Missionary

Pia took advantage of me from the beginning. "Let us pray," she said to me. And I had no place to turn. She installed herself next to the bed and prayed devoutly. She'd let her hair down and it fell past her waist. Pale, always plump, she looked at me and, lowering her eyelashes, pointed to the image of the Virgin and the children of Fatima. Her rolled-up miniskirt drove me crazy and, worse yet, she wore no underwear. "Cover yourself up," I told her. She answered, "Let us pray."

Pia was Catholic by birth. So was I. But she'd found her way into the world beyond, she'd had a good look around and thought it was all fine. I skipped the trip and spent my boyhood masturbating and confessing, out of Grace, worried about veils and sculptures. "Let's go to mass," she ordered. Pia *knew* what went on on the altar, why a crime was committed, against whom, why all the blood, what had to be done to wash the lamb, discover the guilty parties and string them up. I, on the contrary, took deep breaths of incense, smelled the perfume of the women and the lilies, kept my gaze fixed on the back of the neck in front of me, watched the communicants as if they were playing some game and tried to guess what they had hidden between their hands. I felt kind of strange. My knees hurt. I stopped going to holy meetings, I listened to everybody else's confessions, I never went inside the curtains. It took years for me to do my penance. Religion sounded like a bad joke.

I decided to go back to the flat on Potrero Avenue, where Veronica had left me, and start all over with Pia collecting mirrors, folding screens, lace curtains, posters, records, fighting at all hours, scratching the walls, dragging ourselves across the floor, drowning ourselves in the bathtub, screaming in the middle of the night until the police came to shut us up with hoses and strait-jackets. One morning, in front of the Italian cathedral, staring at the yellow walls, the gold dome, the little square with its painted green lawn, I had a vision. The old Italians, in short black jackets and baggy pants, took their hats and flew up in the air, chirping like happy birds. The clean cold wind off the bay carried them over the trees just like dark kites. I, in my strait-jacket, freezing cold, my hair soaking wet, my hands tied, looked up toward the steeples and saw the church collapse like an old wedding cake and shatter at my feet. The Italians swooped down and picked up the pieces, flying up again beating their wings hard. Pia appeared and started scaring them off, shaking a rolled-up copy of the *Corriere della Sera*. This bugged the fluttering Italians. Feathers flew. They honked. Then the cathedral rose up again, but now lit from the inside, with liquid walls and felt-lined doors, and the bells wagged like tongues out of the steeples. The old Italians had turned to jubilant pink-cheeked children, dressed in white robes, carrying garnet flags, gold candelabras and blue votive lamps. A gigantic animal with wings and golden hair came toward me, and hanging in the air waved a censer at me. I went up the steps slowly scattering smoke and blessing the firemen and policemen watching me. The Archangel flew over the courtyard, sheathed his sword and, facing me, took a trumpet out of his back pocket. Then he started shooting and, under the shower of sparks, I went into the church and the altar was shining like a boat on the sea at night. I mounted with sure steps, opened the little door, crossed the presbytery, leaped onto the altar and lay down, covering myself with the starched sheets. Then I fell fast asleep.

My religious crisis was filled with a single voice: a rough

song that rose out of my bed and stuck to the mirror. My soul was like the corner of a jungle. I advanced like a man with a machete: cutting off limbs. Or as an archivist: I dissected Pia, glued her labia together, stuffed Veronica's mummy with sawdust and horsehair. I put on the khaki blouse of the concentration camp, threw my things in a suitcase and headed for the Mission. I disappeared for good. I was finally a missionary. Pia went into a convent in Sausalito.

Sacred History

In those years, around mid-century, a sect called The Flower Children appeared, without commandments or gospels, without churches or orders, a religious sect but musical and free, known by its appearance (hair and smell), not by acts of judgment and prohibition.

Its members went out in the streets and stayed there. They came from the sea but they were looking for the dry heat and open sun of the Pacific. They'd passed through the damp woods of Point Reyes, through the fog of Inverness and the ocean of Tiburon, famous for their braids of seaweed and cellophane, their canned sardines and condoms, and they began to come up from Bolinas to Sausalito, but the hills turned out to be unavailable since they were already taken by executives and architects who defended their property with mudslinging catapults. They were tricked by the slopes of Corte Madera: under the dry fields nuclear weapons were hidden.

The children first occupied abandoned rafts and houseboats. There were sudden shipwrecks, arson and murders. They kept coming and arrived in San Francisco in the summer. They came barefoot, showing off long robes, loaded down with necklaces and amulets. With his horse's eyes and stride of a cat, Allen Ginsberg came leading the way. They founded a mosque called Haight Ashbury and they preached. They were joined by other tribes and other sects. The group looked like a gathering of horseless cowboys, hairy bikers with lion teeth and barebacked women, banjo players and young homosexual couples, Indians with big dark faces and deserters of exotic far-off wars with socks around their necks like 1914 pilots, young Puritans from New England, Quakers and Mormons, floating in their long black cloaks and felt hats and feathers; and drummers from the Fillmore came to join them, long-legged locksmiths from South San Francisco driving their vans held together with ashes and spit, Berkeley chemists armed with sugar grenades—all with the aim of putting some passion in the landscape.

That is, the sect opened like a flower and into it, into its crown, came the suckers, the biters, the lickers, every one with his tongue and her hunk of soul and their degree of love; they climbed the neighborhood stairs, spread out their blankets, covered the windows, hung up their syringes ready to prove that the planet is an open hole if it's peaceful and that people should touch one another and interpenetrate with sweetness and abandon and give themselves to each other since life is an eager adhesiveness and love gives us the necessary depth to identify with each other, in spite of everything, to grow and fill up our emptiness with the infinite goodness of creation. Happiness again will be the space between stars, people and beds.

The children were taken care of like free disciples of a loving Christ, illuminated, like another kid who's going to be crucified and knows it already. Christ, who ascends among soap bubbles, who runs naked through the park and gazes at the flowers through eternity. Christ, who unfolds his cape to play bullfight with the sun at twilight and smells the bonfires among the trees and stays alone and comes home smoking, one step at a time, tired but happy, without knowing what's happening to him.

The Government decided to exterminate this sect. On the day of the innocents, the Vigilantes came out and covered the city with tear gas; they shot at anything moving, killing pigeons and painters alike, in defense of what's essential on this planet. But the sect resisted. Because the sect wants nothing. It acquires nothing and will never acquire a thing. The children make their clothes out of leftover theater props, they go barefoot, they let their bodies and souls grow freely. If there's peace, there's no army; if I do nothing, I create no smog; if I don't kill birds or fishes, we'll have springtime. What's essential on the planet yells: overpopulation, superproduction, fatten the earth! The children look and puke.

One afternoon a Human Be-in was held in Golden Gate Park. Later, various invaders entered the country. This happened in the summer of 1969. The essentials of life went to the Moon to open beer cans and toss them out with the rest of their personal trash. Other important events of that year included: the My Lai massacre, the turning of the ocean into oil, the departure of the whales from the earth.

Meanwhile the Golden Gate opened and in came the children with their long hair streaming in the wind, all kinds of skirts and hats, followed by large groups of older people in heat. The vast meadow was covered with smoke and the smoke, rising, created light, more and more light, and the ocean started to make its rounds, not in the crowd but behind it, taking the brownskinned drummers by the waist and spraying them with foam. The children's children danced hand in hand in the same round of the sea, while horses stamped and pounded the ground with their hooves in rhythm and bicycles leaned against the wall. Photographers shot off their flashbulbs, fists in the air. The circle was closing with all its powers of beauty and truth, the head and the tail tangled together, and men and women, side by side, caressed each other's kidneys and were equal. Man disappeared in woman and woman in man because the community suddenly consisted of just one member, and God looked down with delight on this sect which passed through the eye of a needle.

But the sect of The Flower Children split up, like so many other sects before and since: one sect perished in Lyndon Johhnson's barbecue; another sect nailed shut the doors and windows of their house and turned to stone, cooking up acids; another sect made up mostly of lost children blew themselves up building bombs; another sect was liquidated in one week by child sharpshooters; another sect was sold to a circus and burned itself out without ever being able to communicate with the zebras and giraffes; another sect still survives on the sidewalks awaiting the arrival of the Messiah, eating flowers, crossing the street from one side to the other carrying signs that say: *To Cuba, To the Ganges, To Biafra*. And they wait for months and years for the truck to come along and stop and take them away.

Another sect went to Chicago and came down from the sky driving a pig and they paraded it and proclaimed it President; they sent Jean Genet fluttering from the tower of the Hilton and Ginsberg naked on a cross of poison gas; this sect closed what was called the classical period of the flowers and opened the era of jails, bullets, gags and chains, which in turn was the era of the Revolution and the beginning of the planet's takeover by youths who will live without raping each other, generating spontaneous assistance, and will be their own gurus without reviling anyone, earning their identity without the aid of photographs, not killing their fathers nor demanding Christ's fingerprints, and they'll finish off the bands of old villains, turning them into simple pillars of smoke floating softly into the afternoon sun. This sect, which invaded Chicago, was slaughtered by a butcher and devoured by a jackal in a judge's robes.

Love, Mute Style

What I haven't said yet is that Tahura sat down in front of a green table and started fishing. Through her fingers passed big fish and medium-sized fish, shellfish with mother-of-pearl shells, green chips, blue chips, red and violet, and a soft ballet got going around her. The whirlpool spun fast. Tahura exuded an enveloping smoke. Trembling behind her, I closed my eyes. In a few seconds the wages of all the masses, baptisms, confirmations and weddings of the congregation were gone. But Tahura wrinkled her brow, leaned over the table, dropped her old ashes and put her silver coins in motion again. With my fingers I stroked the person she was sitting on: leathery, like me, tired like me, abstracted, with a taste of iron in his mouth, hopeful, opening to swallow, like me.

But then the difference came clear: the house was glass on the outside and steel on the inside. Tahura touched a bell and the whole house lit up with colored lights and other bells answered and streams of coins came pouring off the roofs. The noise and the glitter lasted a few minutes. Then the house began to breathe. For breathing—through all its halls, its rooms, its restaurants, its toilets, its banks and cash registers—the house had little machines marked with astrological signs, and next to each of these lungs an old woman stood guard at the first sign of fatigue; the old women lowered their bars and turned on the

115

rainbows, the bells rang, the silver rain poured down, Tahura's womb warmed up, blood rushed into the walls and the house breathed. The house, then, was a body, a beautiful big warm body, stinking with light, with felt and money, and this body began to steal Tahura from me.

I wanted to marry her but she had her doubts. I laid my fortune at her feet: it wasn't big enough. I used religious arguments. She listened to me with interest but went off with someone else. She wanted to punish me, crush me. Where was she hiding? The other man sat her on his lap and played her like a guitar. They rolled around on the floor and lost my money hand over fist. They threw me out of the apartment then, and while I manufactured more bills and spent hours hitting the wineskin, they were lying there stretched out naked on the floor face to face, caressing each other's hair, but they couldn't get happy. In fact, they were bored. She and I both knew he was a halfwit: gentle, not violent at all, a beautiful halfwit with delicate hands, curly hair and green eyes, who went through life doing and undoing women little by little, as if they were knots. We loved him. He ate with us, I sang and he danced. He laughed a little; his laugh was that of a mute, you throw sand in their eyes when they're sleeping and they make a noise like "father." We threw sand and he jumped up moaning in his underwear. Then she thought about him a long time: he was a beautiful mute, small and slender, golden like a little bullfighter, with tight calves and a cute ass. I understood. I left the room and set about washing the dishes. They stiffened up, one facing the other, on the floor, like a couple of coffins.

Anyway, Tahura went off with the mute. They left on a train one evening headed north. I saw them go off and I understood, for the first time, what love was. Because I learned how to sound like a mute, to laugh like him, in a sort of death rattle, I learned how to wake up at night with sand in my eyes, to put a guitar on my lap and play her, my Tahura, made entirely of strings, of voices, of panting on the dark hill, flattened among the eucalyptus; I learned to watch her through the lace curtains and look for her in the empty patio, sticking to the damp branches like a snail; I learned to make like rain on the window, and to be like the empty bench where Tahura was waiting for me, but she'd gone.

Law and Order

When Tahura came back she had two kids. Busy with my duties running from jail to jail recuperating alcoholics, drug addicts and epileptics, with the smell of amoebas stuck to my shoes, it was hard to live with Tahura and her family. So we lived apart. I on Potrero Avenue; she in a house with quiet people, given to looking out through the skylight to observe the secret maneuvers of the neighbors. Noises got soaked up in the blue carpet and the cream-colored walls. Between the vines and leaves of the philodendrons, the mailman left little messages and little streams of dark water ran out under the doors like strong tea. Tahura had changed visibly and invisibly. She couldn't smile because an operation on her face had taken out all the wrinkles. Her eyes had reddened and she carried them around in some glass beads that made her cry. Her hair was very blond, like molasses beaten into big waves that came down over her shoulders. I forgot to say that her skin was very tan and weathered, especially on her throat and forearms, but her freckles lit her up so she didn't look too old. I also forgot to say that she received me wrapped in a pink see-through dressing gown under which she was naked. She walked like a cloud in a haze of veils, making a boat-like sound. She seemed to me somewhat overstated, but I kept quiet and waited.

While I was waiting, she rolled some joints. She passed me

one and the grass began to envelope her and then, when I handed it back, I could see big holes in her face, her belly and legs. I leaned back and took a good look at her big loose pussy with its red hair and dark tongue. Its battles had left their mark. A lot of fighting had gone in there, a lot of shooting and a lot of shelling, beachheads, shipwrecks and executions. And some kind of tired truce. Her thighs still looked intact: cool and smooth. I put on my glasses to see better and with my fingers I started prying her open, a little at a time, very gently and precisely, without overlooking the slightest detail. I recognized her moles, her scars, the soft shining fur over the reddened cracks of the English, the tracks of false teeth that had done their damage, the first folds, the pink ear, the live wet shell and the moist secluded oyster gazing out at me. I got down on my knees, put away my glasses and snuffed out the joint. Then Tahura surprised me. She rang a little bell and the room started slowly turning, with the same sounds as a sick person in bed, plus the gears and pulleys of a stage set, and suddenly we were facing a big mirror lit up from inside, where a very tall blonde was lying on her back waiting for a skinny dark man, in boots and a cloak, to start whipping her. The man looked at me and we smiled. Then he began to flick, softly at first, her hips and thighs; she started yelling and twisting in a way that didn't relate to such light blows. Then the man gave her a terrific lash on the twat and she opened her eyes wide. We watched him doing it. She put things into her body: jewelled tubes with vibrating motors, hands full of rings, painted fingernails, mustaches, noses, all damp and drooling and sweet. And she jumped from one mirror to another leaving something like a comet tail in the air. The man handed me the whips and indicated with his mouth where I should strike, I returned his look and seemed to know who he was, now she turned around in the deepest part of the mirror and looked at the reflection of her mouth, her red tongue, her sweaty forehead and her hair down over her eyes. Then she lifted her hand and yanked on a velvet cord. The room opened up and left us under the stars.

In the middle of the bed, with a hard-on, half in, head thrown back, eyes closed, teeth clenched, one hand shaking and waving, the other a fist, riding Tahura like a cowboy, there I was, the same as always, coming not in her but into the sky, casting my seeds from horizon to horizon, rocking like a wind-shaken tree that had survived in spite of everything.

Mirage

Taking everything into account, Tahura worked hard but not hard enough. Since she was still a young woman, one could assume she'd be able to work for twenty more years. Unfortunately, after a day of work and steady whipping, she needed a long rest to pull herself together—let's say six months or so—so that, considered objectively with all due calculations, Tahura hadn't really worked that much in the years I hadn't seen her. Her income wasn't much and her hospital expenses were tremendous, unpayable.

But I'm thinking it's not the work, no, nor the money either; it's a sense of my vocation and of personal realization through chaos. "In this chaos, my love," I say to her, "you'll wake up one day beaten to a pulp."

"You don't understand," she says.

"How don't I understand? I see your bruises, the bites, the scratches, the open wounds, don't I? One day someone will come from some unknown place, speaking a language you've never heard; he'll take off his clothes, leave his robes, rings and turban on the floor, put on his silver spurs, take his scimitar in his right hand and start modeling you like a sculptor does with a lump of clay, and he'll never come but you will and you'll beg him, crying, to come too but the prince won't hear you, he'll go galloping into your dunes with the sand stuck in his eyes and his horse all swollen between his legs, lathering and foaming, and you'll feel his tail tightening around your neck and you'll try to scream but you won't be able to, you'll only hear the chop chop of the machete and the horse's hooves pounding along your flesh. You won't enjoy it anymore, my dear, you won't even be able to cry the way you like to, or put your little hand between your legs or wiggle your little fingers ever again, you won't be able to play with your vibrator and the pounding will have rounded out your face forever."

"I'd like to do it with the dog but he's too big," she answers, "I'd have to cut off his hind feet. Or stick a live rat inside me and let him take a few laps. Anyway, I guess I'll settle for a man. I'll make him a little corner in the mirror, that's where his plate will be, his piece of rug; he'll have plenty of food and water, my little doggy, and the place will be all his."

So the man lived happily inside the mirror: he breathed good air because the mirror was in a flowery corner of the jungle and from its depths rose a lemony scent and a taste of anise; velvet and straw flowers, tied with gold ribbons, covered his head and shoulders, and blue glass or red ceramic candles lit up his eyes. A gesture from Tahura, a striking of the clock, and a door would open and the pet potentate, fat and bald, would enter the mirror wearing red shoes and aluminum clothes, his mouth full of dollar bills, exhausted, and he'd bend over while Tahura covered him with her body and rubbed him up and down with cattle prods. Then he'd have to lie down on the black quilt, feel the cool touch of the sheets, have a smoke while looking at the ship's lantern, catch a whiff of the rain or the wind from the port and wait. Sometimes the plate was empty. Or Tahura, crying and helpless, would leave her things all over the floor, on the bed, on the chairs and in the toilet. Her eyelashes fell off and she wept a black liquid that ran down over her lips, her blond wig slipped down her neck, her breasts hung on their perch and you could see the drops of sweat on her face from a long way off.

But the potentate ran away and, with night falling now, the

mirror opened up and filled with the nice lights of the sunset, the sound of cars, of horns and tires on the avenue, a big ship's siren going by the window, the smell of grilling meat, and Tahura rearmed, fresh and seductive, with her new eyelashes and her refilled breasts and her platinum wig and her heavenly pajamas. In the corner of the mirror she left me a bottle and, closing my eyes, I drank.

But (another but) something had built up between the trainer with the chair in one hand and the whip in the other and that man caged in the mirror—something hard to explain. It was that their skin was wearing out, without peeling off completely, and a smell was coming from inside, making itself felt in a sickeningly sweet way which, once you noticed it, was astonishing because in the smell other nights could be recognized: the sweaty sheets, the basket of dirty clothes, the smell a head left inside a hat. To smell that smell was to feel pity and compassion and, weeping again, find him sitting alone inside the mirror.

Tahura defended herself with masterful gestures. She stood facing me, she looked herself over in me and played with her eyes, her breasts, her belly, her legs; she tickled herself, she wiggled, she wrote herself down and drew herself, she smoked herself out, she turned herself on and off, she lit herself up and brushed out her hair and finally, eyes shining triumphantly, stuck out her tongue at me.

Who or what was there, behind or in that mirror?

"It's not you I love," she said, "but what you put on and what surrounds you, not you but your woman, the woman in you, the woman in you in me. Look."

It was an order. The man looked and what he saw was disturbing: he saw a cardboard forehead, a fat nose and sagging cheeks, pointed teeth, a hairy crotch and two knees. She came into my mirror, ardent, excited, dressed for me, and she let my trembling fingers undo her clothes. We drank and we ate, hours and days flew by in lovely picnics beside the window, playfully tumbling and laughing when one of her legs flew out of the mirror. We were sorry, though, when the distance started to come between us, when an intense preoccupation with her own obscurity clouded her vision. Then Tahura dried up and the desert burned her with a black sun; her eyes fogged over, her skull shrank, her hair fell out, a terrible pain shot through my side and we threw off our clothes in all directions. She kicked, she screamed, she clawed the pillows and threw herself against the wall and stayed there, stunned, huddled in the corner, panting. I couldn't touch her; it filled me with tenderness and pity; I tried to speak to her but she bit me. I backed off then, with my hair on end, and the few things I could offer her from my stomach fell on the floor.

"Get away," Tahura said, and the man crawled back into the mirror with his tail between his legs.

Siamese Twins

One day the potentate brought Tahura a present and this present marked the end of my imprisonment. "I didn't forget your birthday," he said to her, "lie down on your bed, close your eyes, like that, don't open them, wait a second." He tip-toed out and, returning, clapped his hands shouting "Now!" Tahura opened her eyes, raised her head and looked. Through the door came a towering woman, dark-skinned, wearing a white turban covered with diamonds; broad bare shoulders, low-cut dress, the black dress wrapped tightly around her long strong legs. She smiled like a dove that's found her snake. She kept coming forward until she stood beside the bed. She took off the turban and threw it on the floor. She stood there waiting. And then you reached out and took her by the waist and pulled her gradually toward you. Yours wasn't really a smile, it was a mouth that kept opening, and into it went the woman, letting herself be swallowed, looking down your throat for the liquid that would strip her; sinking, turning a little, adjusting her chest and her shoulders to your gullet, shifting her hips in such a way that you could take her in all the way until she disappeared, but you didn't even want her and you let her fall off to the side, lightly. Part of her fell in my mirror and I could smell and touch the inside of her thighs, which she lifted toward me in an arc, opening them wide, so together we could have a look inside her, and you could pass your bejewelled hands and I could pass my hairy ones through the water she was holding back more anxiously all the time. Then she looked like half a woman with a disappeared head, her neck stuck in you, a vein bulging, and she moaned begging me but you wouldn't let her go; you confessed in her ear and set about digging your knee into her and smoke started rising from the friction so you bent down and stuck your face in the fire to put it out. By now she filled up the whole room thrashing at the waist from side to side; the idols you'd stashed in her pussy fell out; and raising herself up like a bridge, supporting herself on her head and heels, she slid toward me and fell and I saw the white dome coming at me on her head, dripping at first, then gushing into a crazy explosion of lights that drenched my mouth, my chest, and made me shut my eyes. But you, wise and slow and persistent, took hold of her again and gobbled her down, making room for her, taking her in so she could hibernate in you, and she tried to wiggle out and fight; but you overcame her, wearing her out, and when you weakened it was she who began to revive you, licking you from the feet up, biting you awake, giving your vagina mouth-to-mouth respiration, breathing you back to life for a long while, in no hurry, rhythmically, until you got back your strength and went back to eating and squeezing, chewing and kissing her.

Sitting in my mirror, trembling, I smoked and let you do your thing. I knew that you were finally finding the food for your solitude and that you'd live, from that night on, split in two, stuffing yourself with the faithfulness and tenderness you deserved. You were a mother, Tahura, the mother of someone who'd rest in your womb forever, someone you would arm and defend, a sweet little lamb in your great solitary motherly lap. You were the master of light and you rightly put me out. You got up from bed, lit a joint, took a long toke, came over to the mirror and covered it with a black sheet. I knew that we'd signed a death sentence. Yours.

Tahura began receiving mysterious long distance phone calls. The voice wouldn't say who it was. It proceeded to insult you and ask about your family.

The Canary's Crime

"It's someone who knows me very well," you said, "who's patiently studied my habits and watched my house and knows where I go, what time I return, who I call, who comes to see me, where I keep my money. He's calm. He insults me intelligently. I can't hang up on him."

"How come?"

"He insults me, but he says it all like a husband to his wife of many years, strong things, said when he's on top of you, caressing you."

"How old is he?"

"I have no idea, nor do I have a clue as to what he does or where he lives or how he finds out what he knows. He calls and he hangs up. It bothers me, it even makes me mad, but afterwards I keep thinking about that voice and sniffing it out as if it were stuck in my throat. Perhaps he calls from his job. I think he works at the zoo because more than once I thought I heard the sounds of animals nearby. He could be playing a record to throw me off, or calling me from a pay phone *in* a zoo. How am I going to figure it out? He asks about the kids. But he doesn't come over. Lately he calls me every day and sends messages printed in block letters which he sticks on yellow paper. I mean this man is like a teapot with no place to blow off steam, a force with no way out that's likely to split his pants. One message said: TO LOVE YOU IS TO CRUSH YOU. That's all. As if I were a can of sardines. The message arrived and the telephone rang. He told me I was a great big whore and that he was watching me from the other side of the street. But when I opened the window there was no one. Now when the doorbell rings, I think of his calls."

It can't be said that I was there when it happened. Understand me clearly: it can't be said I was there. Nevertheless, I can suggest a few clues, offer certain descriptions, give a fair idea of the layout of the place and even organize a sort of schedule of events. None of this implicates or complicates me. Consider it a public service.

The bell rang. Tahura left her glass on the table, got up, walked over and opened the door. A tall man stepped in like a big buzzard, a dark type, no hat, dressed in a frogman suit with goggles on. He gave Tahura a shove and she fell at my feet. Or what could have been my feet. One can't be certain of any details. The frogman grabbed Tahura by the throat, picked her up and slammed her against the stereo. Tahura started bleeding from the nose. The frogman folded her in half, punched her in the face, spread her out on the couch and fucked her fast, saying short sentences, giving orders, naming names. It seemed to me Tahura was looking for my throat. I didn't know if she wanted to speak to me or bite me. She was drowning in blood. And was fighting now with a strength that, really, could hardly have been expected of her. She bit hard. She sunk her nails in; the frogman's suit shrieked but it didn't break. It was his best defense. Then I realized that I was standing there with the glass in my hand. I smashed it against the wall and the shards fell at my feet. The frogman chased Tahura through the kitchen and tried to catch her with a steel hook; she got away, but pieces of her stayed on the hook. As a door slammed open, I saw silverware, bottles and tools flying through the air. Then I saw them in the corridor in a strange tete-a-tete because they seemed to be keeping time to a record on the stereo and Tahura was spilling herself out, her face covered with blood, while the frogman pounded her down with punches to the head and belly. Tahura sank her nails into the wall and looked out, between her hair, at the hook keeping time like a baton conducting a dance. Then there was a silence. I mean, I heard at my feet a slow splash, which was Tahura falling into the blood puddle, and in my ears the breath of the frogman who was drowning and couldn't keep his throat from gurgling with a flute-like whistle. Then he tried to walk out and he stumbled and his rubber feet sucked at the floor. He hacked the door open with an ax, balanced himself on the bed and started punching the pillows, which were also filling with blood. Suddenly he went back into the kitchen and looked in the cupboards until he found a rope and went wandering all over the house with it, making a necklace out of what he was trying to keep forever, like the memory of his last dance at the bottom of the sea; and on the necklace he strung the chair and the lamp in the corner where he read, the blue bottle, the guitar he played alone in his room, the tortoise-shell portrait and the wax flowers, one knot for Tahura and two little ones, like on a rosary, for the children, and finally he was stringing out his debts, his letters, until he struck blood and couldn't link it up and started blowing bubbles with it like a glassblower and the bubble got bigger and bigger, filling the rooms, the hallway, the kitchen, the living room and the stairs, the walls and the ceiling, and inside the red phosphorescence he sat down and looked at his hands, not moving, because the window was open and through it the incredible bubble gently floated away.

The Clues

It's absolutely necessary to seek out a few clues that can help us all, you as much as me, and this isn't easy because, since then, there's been no clear sense of order in this house and it's not even certain that such clues, if found, would prove useful.

The clues, then!

I remember clearly an evening or morning of sunless light, round and even light, like from an opaque reflector, but intense, the kind of light occasioned by an eclipse as long as this eclipse doesn't mean clouds passing swiftly across the sun but something completely static, giving a special sense to what one sees. I climb a hill and I notice that everything's burned to a crisp. I keep climbing. What I feel isn't exactly anguish, it's more like astonishment. Because before I get anywhere I know perfectly well that it's not just the hill that's been fried but the whole world. On reaching the ridge, certain things occur which can't be given much importance because they're typical of dreams: I have to scratch and claw my way uphill, below I can see a precipice. I manage to reach the edge and, with one last push, I fall headfirst into the chasm—but I don't fall; I find myself between two rocks, passing from one precipice to another, knowing that I still can't give up.

Then there's the memory of a night when my company has to take off in helicopters. We leave our cave and up we go. Then something very quick and beautiful occurs: in one leap I go flying at great heights in a capsule that leaves only my head free; the sky is very blue and the stars move off into the distance; then come a couple of dizzying maneuvers: an ascent and a gliding curve. I feel the cold night on my face and the sweet heat of the capsule wrapping me from feet to throat like a mummy.

The following clues are more emotional and I beg your patience, your understanding.

When Tahura went off with the mute, it was no trick, it wasn't the thing that husbands suffer when they see the closet empty and the front door ajar. I knew they'd gone and, seeing the train they'd left in, I had a suffocating sensation; I felt that the world had suddenly opened up and that in this break I could never again put anything of mine; that we'd been split up and she'd thrown my face into the void in such a way that we'd never get it back, neither she nor I. It was absolutely determined, something against which I'd always be powerless. Quickly I began to make telephone calls to everyplace at all hours. No answer. I sent messages. I thought I'd be able to take off too and follow them. Get to where they were, knock on the door, throw myself on the floor and wait for them, beg them, crying. But at the same time I realized that I still *didn't know* where they were and would never know. I'd lost them completely. But it wasn't so. Because years went by and, little by little, building a little spider web in my bed, putting bars on the skylights, tied to the table with my plate bolted to a chain hung from my neck, contrite before the children who looked at me very curiously, I was being made to forget my little wife, and, while she was making me forget and feeling my face, my eyebrows, my mouth with her fingers, she was also scratching at the ground around me and, later, digging under my feet. My first discovery: my legs had been shortened and my chest had grown noticeably, a bag formed in my belly, I started getting a new sense of my clothes, strange things were growing out of my back. With a snap, like an elastic band that comes loose and whacks us in the face, the 25-year contract appeared, renewable, which we signed more or less as is. Frightened, I considered my situation. I was connected to an elegant piece of furniture, fragrant and very colorful, but my bed was a hospital bed, the sheets had the marks of a mortal combat, my gown was a straitjacket.

The worst was yet to come.

I found out in a way I can't reveal that my little wife, at some very real and specific time, had had a lover to whom she was bound by love. By love, for godsakes! A lover she caressed, kissed, bit and wet with the juice I never knew; a lover who, when the time was ripe, overcame her and me both. She declared simply: "I must follow him." She said it sadly but firmly. And they disappeared. And later she came back. Everything went on the same: the same little spider web, the same white bed, the same rumpled sheets, the smell of night, the shape of my pants, the yellow stew, the children grown up, her wrinkles stuffed behind her ears, her flaming hair, and me trembling on my weak legs.

One more clue: I remember entering the apartment and in bed was my little wife, naked, asleep. I noticed that her breasts had grown and that they were shaking steadily. On the other side of the flat, on the sofa, I saw a stranger. Also naked. Suddenly the stranger went over to the bed, first next to my wife; then he stuck his head under the bedclothes and all I could see were his hairy legs. And there he was again with his face next to my wife's, his eyes wide open and his hands behind his head. I asked her if she wanted to stay with the stranger and, half opening her eyes, she said yes, for a while, that later she'd come over to me. I stammered something but she didn't understand what I said. Then another woman I know, but I won't say who it was, said to me: "There's nothing you can do, get out of here."

This last clue hasn't been repeated. On the other hand, I've learned to live with the other one: I know for certain, with the certainty of a condemnned man, that my wife had that lover, hidden from me, but knowing that I knew, and that it lasted for some time, and that Tahura came back, the great Tahura, and I know and I'm forever sorry, but I don't know when it happened, nor with whom, even though the lover seems sort of familiar. I look at her and it leaves me with a tremendous retching of grief, without knowing whether I should take her again right here, as always, or whether to start strangling her as I should.

The last clue is simply a rainy afternoon: I go out in my slicker, with my hat over my eyes and a scarf at my neck, I pass by a tree and I see a couple. They're very young, she has coppery hair, he's dark; water runs down their faces, they hold their island without armies; he puts his arm around her waist; the water rises over their ankles; the trees are bending under a furious wind; rain whips the walls; a yellow bus comes wobbling along, rolling from one side of the street to the other; the sky darkens; I jump aboard the bus and look back, the shipwrecked ones are smiling at me, and, as I move off, the water covers them completely.

Purgatory

I was summoned to a Vigilante Court. From the start I understood they were out to get me. There's no proof I ever came here, nor that I lived in my apartment, nor that my family exists. They deny that my furniture's in the cellar, that I was an executioner, a teacher, a photographer, that Cuzco, Veronica, Judith, Rosamel, Pia and the Monk, whom I want to present as friendly witnesses, ever shared this house with me. They've got a file on me.

The session was on the landing, in a large brightly lit concrete bunker, with seven seats for the vigilantes, a cot covered with a sheet, rubber hoses and a machine I couldn't identify. To get there from my floor, I went through twelve electric doors: one electronic eye let me go through and another shut the doors behind me. Obviously there was no going back. The population of the country, interested in alternatives to war, attended this interrogation crammed in elbow to elbow behind barbed wire. It's safe to say we're in a stadium and that these people, whom I don't understand and whose ways I find distasteful (they've come to stuff themselves with hot dogs and drink beer by the bucketful), prefer a hopeless case and a death sentence to an unclear case in which the vigilantes might recommend an acquittal.

I'm seated on a bench, under a powerful searchlight, facing thousands of sergeants with their hats on and their wives whose shackles have been removed. I'm accused of having entered an apartment, barricaded the door and beaten a woman to death. I say that when this happened I was at the front. It is proved to me that on that date I couldn't have been at the front because I'd already been discharged and that was the day I'd disappeared, leaving a few receipts of recent transactions in my room. Charges and pleas follow.

My position is clear and firm. I declare the following:

First: The war produced in this house a frightened and hypocritical race corrupted by shame, a race that renounced the country's church and religion and which participated in the latest attempted murder of God, for which they tried to place the blame on some German typographers.

Second: This country is the creation of a computer recently built by some rude drunks named Teller, Von Braun and Katz—men who brought the wrong tools over from Europe, forgot important parts and, in moments of alcoholic expansiveness, fed the computer lysergic acid.

Third: Said computer was programmed by Hitler, Goebbels and Count Ciano during seances. So that in an early phase of the program the master race wins the World War and accuses God of suicide; the new generation is sterilized with milk; iron chastity belts are manufactured, the universities teach musical masturbation, the churches close on Sundays. In the second phase, old people no longer die. In the third phase, young people don't fit in at home, the computer makes a mistake, endorses free love and the world fills up with pregnant bellies.

Fourth: The Vietnam war is programmed. But the computer's programmers haven't considered certain side-effects. For example: the country produces antibodies; the Chinese bottle the yellow peril and export it freely by sea; next to the red peril rises the black peril and, being hard to bottle since it ferments so fast, it absorbs the others and the computer begins to split its sides, starts shuddering and spitting, jumps out of its puddle and blows its fuses.

The Vigilantes strike my testimony with one stroke. They take me by the arms and hustle me through corridors full of reporters who rush after us, there's a brief scuffle, I let out a howl and disappear down the tunnel into the locker room.

Spirit of Evil

Serenely I sit and reflect, going over my thoughts: outside it's winter, without surprise I've watched how everything's gone on dying; I saw the sky turn to a violent forge, the whole sunset reddened so the world glowed and the marks of the bars stood out on my hands; the sea roughened, floating on its back, shifting its weight from one wave to another, lonelier and larger all the time, below my cell. I understood what was beginning to happen to me in this city forever at war.

To remain alone, to make your payments, to wake up one evening with a dog licking your face: all this is part of living in this house. At night I wander through the corridors turning on lights, closing doors and windows. I set up chairs like traps; I leave four swords beside the bed, along with a glass of water and my poisons. Everything's ready: my house is surrounded by squad cars in the dark; the assassins are studying my windows; when drowning in my blood, I'll take communion calmly; the knife blades crackle all night, and at the foot of my bed there's a suicide spread-eagled.

This section of the city—where a man lives with a strange sensation in his throat, loses his hair and grins while his chest comes loose, where he bends over to eat with bored shoulders and everything turns to bile in his mouth, and, seeing his wife naked, he begs for his wine bottle—was taken by force several years ago. It happened suddenly and left us no time to clear our minds. The bishops fell; cameras were installed on the altars, in tombs and in banks with the aim of catching God by surprise—or his Son, at least. People took off their clothes on the streetcars and armed police were replaced by fakirs; original sin was taken in pills; the sky was painted black; we crawled up the walls and mystics got married; we saw stark-naked virgins jumping out of windows with toothbrushes in their mouths; truckloads of symphony instruments were mysteriously hijacked; physicians drove out to the desert and shot themselves; children fell straight from their mothers' wombs into the void; soldiers would wander nostalgically away from the battlefront, pull stockings over their faces, climb onto balconies and begin shooting. But most serious of all, and what's truly chilling, which I have to set down here in writing, is the presence of a power, an embodiment of evil, a kind of hunter who takes over the city and commits his crimes for two reasons: one, because the safety valves on all the teapots in the house broke at the same time and, consequently, the transition between murder and peacefulness is eased; and two, the man makes no distinction between a massacre and celebration, he likes to kill; it's simple, like hunger and thirst and happiness.

Or put it another way; the hunter carries armloads of funeral flowers, wears peace beads and war beads around his neck and bandanas around his head; he trims his fingernails with a sharp knife, worships his beard and his smell of leather and underwear, fornicates and masturbates continuously, and transports his family in a van.

Among his various ritual acts, he committed his now-historic murder. Disguised as a cowboy, with long hair and glassy beads, he put his family in their van and drove around the city in search of a cemetery. He found one, stopped the car, they got out, cut the telephone lines, climbed the fence; a car was coming out, they killed the driver with a single shot and entered the house; in the living room they saw a Polish man lying down; further inside, in a bedroom, they found a pregnant actress and, next to her, a hairdresser fixing her hair; and in another room, also in bed, a coffee heiress was reading and she waved to her murderess; then, the party having started, they shot the Pole twice in the back; the heiress was stabbed in the face and chest; the actress died with her throat cut without having to see her baby shot; they tied her neck to the hairdresser's, hung them both from a beam and opened his guts with a screwdriver. Having lost track of herself in the world's eyes, one young murderess, also pregnant, returned to the scene of the crime, took a towel, dipped it in the actress's stomach and, with this improvised brush dripping blood, proceeded to paint PIGS on the door of the house.

The hunter and his family went back to their lair, lit their kerosene lamp, built a fire on the floor, opened their canned goods and ate their sardines and drank their Cokes. In the firelight, pensive, they saw the cardboard coyotes, the wooden horses, the wax sheriff and the plastic hanged men at the opening of the movie. The hunter scolded his family. He accused them of being violent and bloodthirsty, cruel and soulless. Cannibals, he called them. Then he ordered them to reflect on his words in silence, paying close attention to the songs he sang them accompanying himself on his guitar.

At dawn, when the film crew arrived and the spotlights reddened the cardboard-rock hills and a storm wind began to pick up out of the portable propellers, the hunter gathered his family, put them in the van and they took off in search of another cemetery. "Now you'll see," he said to them, "you're children of God and not of Satan." He led them to the door of an ivy-covered house, rang the bell, stepped inside, took the man of the house into his bedroom, tied him down and blindfolded him; he led the woman of the house to another room and covered her face; then he sang them a pretty ballad and, still singing, stuck a fork into each of them until the old folks opened like faucets.

The hunter drove his family home, had a little dispute with a customer in one of the local cafes, killed him with one shot and buried him under the sheriff's window. Then he announced he was going away for a couple of weeks. His trip coincided with the appearance of some bold ads in the papers. One of them said:

"This piece of shirt belongs to the taxi driver killed by me with a bullet in front of City Hall."

Another:

"Hairs illustrating the murder of the young woman stabbed while making out with a young man beside the river."

The hunter's family read the ads while stirring their cornflakes in cold mother's milk. The hunter, for his part, furious over the cynicism of the police, who insisted they were on the killers' trail, presented an official statement to the Supreme Court, from which I excerpt the closing passages:

"Death is the goal of the age of love. I gather grieving souls, orphans, unwed mothers, sweethearts, all dropped out of a life that only knew how to crucify lovers.

"Your honors, jailers and executioners of a humanity that drinks blood and eats from the Father's side, I am the liberator, the power that gives eternal life, the builder of bodies, the shepherd of the flock of happy slaves.

"Let the bodies come to me.

"Follow me, slaves, to the sea of light. Rest on my lands, roast lambs. Don't despair. To die is to love me."

Eternal Return

My defense is becoming clear. I won't see summer. I've placed my bed by the window. I'm alone. Around me friends and family are dying. I know all the secrets. Nothing and no one surprises me anymore. The world is bright and transparent. My days are like little glassy ponds where a fish is swimming in front of a mirror. I know where the fern and the quartz are, the window and the three walls; I think I know the line where the water ends and the sky begins, at least I can feel where the air's stopped for me. Facing my bed, touching the fake glass of the window, there's a cheerful branch of camellias, and next to it, climbing the beams, a vine and, facing them, the cups of the magnolia full of rain. All this and the pines, the dark loquat, the clouds, and red berries of the pyracantha, the flight of the pelicans, the step of the cat, the gray rounds of the pigeons, the heads of the children, everything ought to be beginning again. I must understand it clearly, take deep breaths, incredulously drink it in and look at you closely, observing the shine of your hair, your eyes in the midday light, your teeth. And you, detached, watching me stick out my tongue, close my eyes, moaning, in love again, languishing and happy, opening you up without running into any buttons or buttonholes, submersing my face in the quiet afternoon, stretching my hands out to have you again.

This is the garden, the sky, the morning, the flowers, you and the children, and yet there's nothing that's ever going to be mine again, nothing's about to change so I can live again and we can once again enter the summer I knew, the love made of streets, of houses, of cars and courtyards where I learned to love myself, and embrace myself and scare myself silly, because the day was in my parents' bed, and my brothers learned to disappear and they kept leaving me the melancholy question, the person who kissed me, who ran away, who threw herself on park benches for abortions and came home wrapped in ether, floating as if she were made of cotton. Everything's here, but it's already passed me by. Some things passed right through me as if I didn't exist, went through and kept on going. I see people I knew well who've died and now surround me sitting in easychairs. An old woman arrives with a notebook of poems and burns it to keep her feet warm. They're real, I'm sure, but they're no good to me now; this afternoon is happening somewhere else. Nothing's going to give anything back to me. Not a step backward, not a leap, no desktop religion. In my room we smell an atmosphere of mattresses. I sing on my back, I read the mail, I invent women, I wait by the window for the new year, but I don't tell anyone; I look outside and the afternoon is empty; I'm not afraid, yet I feel a great sadness, I'd like to organize my death: to know if they burn you with your shoes on or if your socks are enough, whether the worms crawl in through the hinges or fall from the silk or come with the coffin, or if they go out through the navel, if they jump in the water, if one summer's long enough to dry you out and then come the blessed plows; I'd like to complete a few years of violence and then follow the schedule of the Benedictines who, as I understand it, stop speaking, sing in the dark and keep a room empty and open for poor God to sleep in, deprived of his little wife and of his Son.

Let's dance! We'll die of Parkinson's disease.

I Am an Optimist

I've said that I moved my bed and raised the pillows. Now I look in the glass for the reason this winter has lasted so long. I wake up at night with my mouth full of handkerchiefs. I cracked my arm reaching for one of the swords. I can feel the breathing of the thieves in the garden. Last night I heard two explosions: one threw flames across the hills, the other came spinning like a burning helicopter and hung a long while over the reservoir before it fell hissing and throwing up clouds of steam and water. There's fighting all over the city. Bombs go off in police stations and squad cars; gasoline shoots from the hoses of the firefighters; there's sand in the presses of the newspapers and acid in the bottles breaking on the soldiers' shields. Quietly the police work the old people over, they drag my children away by the hair and haul the girls off by the legs; black panthers are tied to chairs, their mouths gagged with rags, their arms and ankles chained; at four in the morning, as in a waltz, the sirens go off, the dogs come out with their dogs, climb the steps and open fire; gentlemen die in their beds, poking their heads out the window, pulling their pants on, looking for their ladies in the dark.

Suddenly more murderers are seen in daylight than at night: they shoot from under the rocks, out the windows of restrooms; they hold group massacres, then split up and kill themselves. A bank president comes to his office window and threatens to jump; they clear the sidewalk, mark the spot with a dollar sign; the banker changes his mind, turns around and falls into a policeman's arms who hugs him passionately.

What's going on? Why this bloody war—flagless, hushed-up, underground—why this handing out and picking up leaflets at night, why do the teachers wear bulletproof vests and their students fall bleeding from the bell towers, how come the city's covered with smoke at twilight and the parks get dug up and a breastless woman is dancing and the historic choruses keep going by, voiceless and noiseless, and the guitars are glowing and people are dancing in the hospitals?

I've bought myself a wig and I stick my head out to look at the sun. I'm not fooling anyone. And I want to proceed with dignity. I know that this can't last. I've spent fifty years filling myself with air and being emptied, I've seen several generations march to the electric chair and the gas chamber; I've counted the people standing in line to jump off the bridge; and I've heard in the early morning the soft whistle of gas coming out of the kitchens of apartment houses; my books are covered with blood; it's twenty-five years since I've spoken with anyone in this house. Everyone's gone. My wife and kids never came. They forgot me and now they eat with their hats on, their feet on the table and the dining room dripping with wine. I've gone through every tomb in the house. I haven't seen a soul. I've gone up and down the elevator: at the top is an individual armed with an arsenal, at the bottom a septic tank. I've asked in countless official requests for a room with a view of the world. The requests that I write never get anywhere, nobody reads them; I go on disappearing.

But I haven't lost faith. I know that outside men are moving through the trees; I can smell the pines and eucalyptus burning and see the smoke signals over the coast range; I know that the gorges are full of thorns, drunken myrrh trees and thick honeysuckle; I know the fog invades us from the sea and cleans the sky for the sailboats coming up the red canals, and I know that at the doors of other houses there are peaceful people sitting in wicker chairs, young boys playing the accordion, men playing dominoes and girls reading. I hear the songs of the flyers heading south and know that there's a place for me among them.

I'll have a home again and in the house my wife cooking and on the carousel the children and the little horses singing their grandpa's waltzes. I know that the night will be made for our embraces and our breakfasts will smell like fresh-baked bread again and in the mornings we'll slice onions and green chiles and the kids will grow all afternoon, and sitting down we'll make plans for improvements in the interior courtyard and as night falls a fire will blaze for the luck of those yet to be born and we'll tuck potatoes into the coals and the sheets will be fresh again and the air crisp and I'll feel it full in my face and we'll go inside, we'll close the door, and you'll slowly undo your dress while I spy on your nakedness.

So everything's going to work out fine. They'll leave me in peace. Today is my sign of the zodiac. The door is open, I go out and wander the floors of the house at will. I go down to the cellar; they're filling it with ice. I touch the walls in search of cracks, holes, false doors. I don't see a soul. The spotlights are still blue, the doors dry, ajar, with their tin numbers. I'm not sure if the sentries are posted on the roof or not. They probably are, because I can hear footsteps.

The Vigilantes studied all my papers, they signed them and put them in a shoebox. I earned my merit badges: in peacetime I was a spy, in war I machinegunned beautiful families and shot my sergeant in the back, I collected heads, I converted to Christianity, I gave up my habits, I was unfaithful to my wife and I hit my mother, I've killed with a knife, with a pistol and with a bottle-cudgel, I watch television attentively and I place ads in the papers. I ask for just one thing since I know the world is beginning to change and once again I'll be a happy fellow, a creative type, a neighbor with a well-set table, a friend of friends. I want them to let me cut down Rosamel and clean Cuzco's machete; I want to put her shoes and stockings on Tahura, gather all her hairs off the floor and stick them back on her head; I want to go singing to my wedding, with new shoes and a lyre in my hand. That will be the happiest day of my life. I'll remember with each step the night I arrived and found myself in this city; again I'll see the tennis courts golden in the afternoon sun, the light in the trees, the fences covered with flowers, the warm tawny hills, the open balconies, the bay and the bridges, the white towers with their bells ringing and the flaming roosters crowing at dawn. I'll come running outside, I'll buy my own beer, I'll toss my coat over my shoulder and go strolling down the Avenue in search of my singing teacher, then I'll buy some hot dogs, walk by the hookers shaking their hands, and sitting on the terrace I'll softly play my drums. No more marriages for me.

Driving the Message Home

It's five in the morning. A Vigilante leans over my face and gently wakes me. I've got my clothes on. Outside four sergeants are waiting. As I'm going out I notice my Bosswoman hiding behind a door. I go on ahead. The corridor gleams. They've laid down a tar carpet. I walk along in silence. We stop in front of another door where a purple and maroon bishop blesses me; I look for his ring to kiss but I can't find it. We go on walking. My body feels light, my head clear, my stomach empty. We step up the pace. I'd like to burst out laughing, clap my hands, say hello to somebody. We turn to the right, then to the left, we go down a slight incline. We've been walking for several hours. We're going uphill again and at the top of a rise in the corridor I begin to make out my family and friends. Everybody's there! Everybody! My father bareheaded, bald, his eyebrow arched, his mouth frowning a little, smoking a yellow cigarette, I recognize his suit and his shoes. He's my size. And my grandfather very bent-over, loaded down with medals, has an open wound over his eye; he's staring at me with his green eyes, not a blink. My uncles stick out their heads: old Uldarico, very tall, wrapped up in a vicuna shawl, with little bits of paper stuck to his cheeks under those tiny blue eyes and spitting through his teeth; Madariaga, with his pants down, hoarse, dragging his feet, pickled; Escala with no legs, just feet, a trunk and a bony little mouth; don Luis, with no eyes and a gold chain across his chest. I turn around and look and there's don Enrique with his throat slit, and the following ladies: Lala, Sara, Eduvigis, Ester, Hortensia, all dressed in black, standing on one foot, turning pirouettes around a bucket. They look at me affectionately and they're shy, but they don't have any eyebrows or lashes. But who cares. The drowned man looks even worse, laid out, swollen, hairless, missing an eye and a foot, four people holding him down. On we go, leaving them all behind. No time to wave goodbye, not even for my stomach to growl. Here we come. At last. From here on I'm on my own.

This is a trick. Are we there? The sergeants stop, snap to attention, salute and withdraw. They disappear into the light, they turn to a thousand blinding lines that end up splintered at the end of the corridors. I sit down on the floor for a minute. I look at my hands, they're dried out, but I like them; they have scars, hairs, moles; I've got tanned leather on my short flat bones. I'm wearing rubber-soled slippers, black pants and a white shirt with the buttons torn off. I touch my chest hairs, I rub myself and scratch myself softly, I start to close my eyes. My Bosswoman has sat down beside me, she's stroking my hand.

"It's all over," she says. "There's nothing more to worry about. You thought we didn't love you, son, but you're mistaken."

"I'm not mistaken, you old bitch, I know you all hate me and how you hate me."

"But if you go upstairs and get promoted, you'll never see me again, you can't complain."

"Will I have a room with a window? Will it face the garden?"

"It'll face the garden."

"Will my family come? I've been waiting so many years."

"Your family is there already."

"You're putting me on, you old shrew, tell me the truth, are they there?"

"They're there, and nothing's going to separate you again."

"How can I repay your kindness, matriarch? You need any rags, wigs, scissors? A war that's lasted this many years isn't so easy to forget."

In the palm of my hand her hand is a snail without a shell, squished and sticking to mine, but not too slimy. I peel it off gently and let it fall between my legs. Her round face, her thick glasses, her blue tongue, everything that's left of her starts laughing and her tits shake under her nurse's apron. I know I ought to excuse myself but I'm not sure how. I'd like to give her a good whack. But I'd rather not mess with her. She sticks a pencil between her teeth. She's stalling. She's going to ask me for money. Me! That hustler. I get up and just start walking. The corridors are the same, same doors, same numbers. Nobody home. They lied to me. I know I don't have the slightest idea of the layout of this house and that I'll never find my way out and will never be able to get back to where I started. Not that I want to go back. But to get there, yes, even if I'm exhausted and my arms hurt and my neck hurts and my back, even if they find me completely bleached-out, my nose swollen, beaten. What's the difference. This is how beaches are when they're not there except in dreams: they're eternally long and blazing hot and they cut our feet with their millions of broken shells and bits of glass; our eyes are burning, our face is peeling and the horseback riders in swimtrunks come galloping along and stop to look us over while their horses roll around in the sand, covering themselves with black kelp and dead octopuses.

But I'm wrong. This is not my destiny. No one condemned me to walk eternally down passages of light and cardboard. There's one door open wider than the others. Mine. I know it's mine. I don't hear any voices or noises. But it doesn't matter. They're waiting for me in there. At last, thank God. I open it slowly, an inch at a time, and go in.

I start up some carpeted stairs and stop when I reach the landing. In front of me on the floor I see a puddle of blood, a thick pool, dry, and in the puddle a pair of women's shoes. On the wall there's a single stain, from top to bottom, someone slid down and crumpled on the floor. But there are hairs too and fingernail marks and signs of a struggle. I pass by quickly, I know I have a strange expression on my face and with my hand I keep on saying no. I go into the living room. Someone's been sleeping on the sofa. There's a bloody handprint on the wall, and more blood on the cushions and on the curtain. I start finding things on the floor. Someone has put them there for my benefit, following a certain pattern. Next to the wall I see a manikin's head, bald, eyeless, the kind they put wigs on to dry in the sun; its lost hairs are real, they're all over the place, black and curly, they stick to my shoes and pants. I open the door to the kitchen and that's a mistake. I walk among broken bottles, silverware, pots and pans strewn every which way; a hammer appears to be hanging in the air. I follow the tracks out into the hall. There are the shoes again and I'm in the bathroom. The sink, the tub and the walls are splashed with red. I see a woman's jacket on the floor, I touch it with my foot, all the buttons have been torn off. I keep looking until I find the children's room with its beds turned down for the night, the sheets immaculate, one pink quilt and the other light blue. I lean against the wall; I'd like to stay here, close a huge door and throw the key away and live here and start all over. But it's no use. I know perfectly well I'm expected in another room, that I can't put it off or escape it, that I'll get there, it's got to be. And I go out into the corridor and head straight for the bedroom, my face and hands feel cold, and a horrible nausea is rising in my chest. Then I run and smash the door and go in. Half the bed is dried blood, the other half a hole where something was buried that's not there. That's where the fists hit, in that wide space, the blows were struck there, thudding against the pillows in slow motion and everything fell slowly through the years and the arms were raised slowly and the hands opened and the screams came muffled out of the old closets beyond all recognizable time and the blood spread out like dead oil forming a pool at the base of a wall that no longer exists.

I know perfectly well I must look very closely everywhere, go over and remember all the details, measure each one and make notes of what I see. It will be necessary to give an account. But I also know there's something more important in this room, and that it's essential to face it, to face you, now and forever, vicious hunter, and there you are looking at me in the mirror with my terror, our anguish and our knives in our hands.

Berkeley, 1967-1970

COVER DESIGN: NARCISO PEÑA